KING OF CUPS

THE TAROT KINGS
BOOK THREE

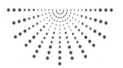

AMY KUIVALAINEN

THE NEW SERENE REPUBLIC

The New Serene Republic

The New Serene Republic of Venice is governed by a Council of Ten, made up of two representatives from each of the four ruling Houses, in addition to the Doge, who is always human, and his Grand Sorcerer. The current Doge is Giordano Loredan, and the Grand Sorcerer is Arkon Ziani.

The Ruling Houses of the Republic

House of Swords

The House of Swords, a.k.a. The House of Air, belongs to the air shifters and is predominately ruled by shedu. The shedu are capable of a human form and that of a winged lion. They originated from Babylon and ruled Constantinople before establishing themselves in Venice in 1562.

With their great wealth and knowledge, they have always helped govern and shape Venice from the shadows. At the dawn of the New Republic, in the year 2103 AD, the shedu were the first shifters to come into the light and take their rightful place on the Council of Ten.

The most prominent family and House of Swords representatives on the Council are the 'Golden-Winged Ones,' Carmella Aladoro and her son, Domenico. The sestieri of San Marco and San Paulo, despite being home to the richest humans in Venice, are shedu and other winged shifter territories.

House of Wands

The House of Wands, a.k.a. The House of Fire, belongs to the Djinn, other creatures of flame, and those who use fire-based magic. Djinn have a pure form that is rarely seen by outsiders, but they can take on a human's appearance when it serves their purpose.

The House of Wands is ruled over by the Djinn King, Zahir Matani, who represents them on the Council of Ten along with his second in command, Ashirah.

Along with the Djinn, the sestieri of Cannaregio and Santa Croce is home to human bankers, money lenders, and any other human or shifter with a fire affinity.

The only part of Cannaregio not ruled by the Djinn King, is the Jewish Quarter that falls under the jurisdiction of the Doge and the Council of Ten.

The Court of Wands monitors their domain by royal boat, which for fire beings proves not only the King's strength but also his authority, and rattling the mettle of those who wish to gain his favor.

The Djinn King is known for dispensing advice, justice, money, and deals to those who dare to consult with him.

House of Cups

The House of Cups, a.k.a. The House of Water, belongs to the sea serpent clans, other water shifters, and humans whose trade relies on the ocean, such as sailors, naval merchants, and fishermen.

They are governed by General Josefina Serpente D'Argento

and her nephew Nicolo, who represent the House of Cups and the Venetian Navy on the Council of Ten.

The sestieri of Castello is their domain along with the islands of San Giorgio Maggiore, Murano, Burano, and Torcello.

The House of Cups is responsible for the policing of all maritime activities and the shipbuilding yards.

Of all the Houses, they are the most militant, running the protection of the New Republic and policing the shipping lines between Venice and New Constantinople.

House of Coins

The House of Coins, a.k.a the House of Earth, is the only House dominated by humans and also accounts for all other types of magic-users, such as sorcerers, artificers, and alchemists. The sestieri of Dorsoduro and the Giudecca is home to scholars, writers, doctors, and scientists.

Their two representatives on the Council of Ten are Lorenzo Tera, an earth mage, and Frederico Romaro, a non-magical lawyer. When the House can't get what they need from their Council members, they often petition the Republic's Grand Sorcerer, who is answerable only to the Doge.

The Grand Duchy of Varangia - Enemies of the Republic

The Varangian Kingdom covers the areas of Eastern Europe from Russia to Romania, but also Hungary, Slovakia, and Poland. Their tsar, Arkadi Vasin, rules from the capital of Volgograd.

The Republic and Varangia have been at war for five years since the Varangians tried to take New Constantinople from the Turkish Empire. Trade partners to the Republic, New Constantinople sought aid from the Venetian Fleet and managed to defeat the Varangians, pushing them back to Romania.

Afterward, the Varangians declared the Republic as enemies and have since been working to take Croatia from Venice's rule. Varangians abhor magic and magical creatures, encouraging the eradication of all non-humans within and outside the borders of their empire.

The Tsar has only one magical advisor: the famed Wolf Mage, rumored to be of Saint Olga of Kyiv's bloodline. The Wolf Mage wields the saint's power against the Republic's Grand Sorcerer and the Republic's army.

AUTHOR'S NOTE

The Tarot Kings world, while based in some respects on medieval Venice, is a fantasy world. This story is a high seas adventure on ships loosely Byzantine in design, but please don't look for any kind of historical accuracy.

I just wanted to write pirates, puffy shirts, sword fights and shenanigans. I am, despite the rumours, only human.

THE GODS OF THE CANALS

Long ago, before Rome's constant wars pushed people to hide amongst Veneto's protected islands, there lived *incolae lacunae*— the lagoon dwellers. They survived and thrived off the bounty of the sea, and they paid homage to Reitia, the sea serpent mother, who protected them in her sheltered waters.

It didn't matter when the golden shedu came from Constantinople or when the grim-faced priests came from Rome. The sea serpents were not only protectors of Venice; they *were* Venice. It was their sharp fanged ferocity and love that kept the whole Veneto safe.

The most powerful of all the serpent families was the Serpente D'Argento. The Silver Serpents believed in trade and democracy, but they believed in Venice most of all. From the doge to the beggar, everyone knew in their hearts that the minute the serpents decided things were not being run properly, there would be no saving the condemned.

Venice was their god, and they served her in the great blue waters of the Adriatic.

Commander Nicolo D'Argento was a prince amongst his

people who would maim, kill, and destroy whatever threatened his city.

The Varangians had been careful to keep their war with the Republic on solid ground, but it wasn't Venice's war ships they feared. It was Nico and the sea serpents he could command.

Just one of the dragons of the sea could turn a ship to kindling, and they delighted in doing it. It was because of their destructive power that the doge kept them on a tight leash.

It was therefore highly unfortunate news for the pirates of the Adriatic to learn that the doge had finally set his feral commander loose on them. The Pirate King had finally pushed the Republic one step too far, and all of them were going to pay.

There was blood in the water.

The Silver Serpent was free to hunt. And not even Fate herself was going to be able to stop him.

CHAPTER ONE

The hot wind blew tendrils of Nico's dark hair free from the knot that held it back from his face. It was the kind of wind that people in Venice saw as a bad omen, and they shut their doors and windows against it.

Nico loved the *sirocco* wind. It held a wildness that whipped up a kind of madness in the men and made them even more vicious in battle. He wanted that ferocity and lack of mercy.

Nico was finally leaving Venice to hunt the Pirate King, and he welcomed the chaos that matched his inner serpent. After months of cat and mouse games, it wanted pirate blood on its fangs.

The *dromon* warship was full of men ready to fight and die for the Republic. Two mages strolled about the deck, making sure that the high winds caught the sails properly and they had maximum speed.

The ship sailed through the blue-gray waters like a blade through butter. They slowed where the lagoon opened out to the sea at the Lido and the two waters met. Nico walked to the front of the ship, carrying a jar of holy water, salt, and a bundle of olive branches. The men all bowed their heads as he tossed the items into the sea as an offering to Neptune, Poseidon, or Saint Nicholas—the saint of the sea—whichever way the men's faith swung. In Nico's mind, it was always to Reitia, the goddess of Venice, who would protect her sons out on the water.

"We pray the sea is always calm and quiet for us and all who sail upon it," he whispered. To his goddess, he added, "Let the hunting be good, and my prey be worthy of the fight."

Nico had heard many rumors about the Pirate King, but sailors were the worst of gossips and superstitious to a fault. If he believed them, the king was ten foot tall and breathed fire. Even Arkon, the supposed spy master of the Republic, couldn't seem to separate fact from fiction. In any case, he was too focused on the Wolf Mage to worry much about bothersome pirates sailing up and down the Croatian coast.

They had been a minor annoyance in the past, but three major acts against the Republic had pushed Nico over the edge. The first big mistake had been when they had kidnapped an artifice inventor and his daughter from a boat carrying them from Constantinople to Venice. The intel they had received afterwards was that the Varangians had been the buyers. The inventor had been working on magi-tech that would create stronger magical-powered engines for warships. Now he was in the hands of Venice's enemies.

The second mistake the Pirate King had made was sneaking a Varangian mage into Venice. Less than a week ago, that blasted mage had almost bound Zahir, king of the djinn, to a ring to take back to his emperor. He had also tried to kidnap Zahir's consort and a brilliant magician, Ezra, to force her to make golem soldiers for the Varangians.

The final mistake had been that the Pirate King had flown Nico's flag so all eyes looked to him. It had been a clusterfuck and an absolute embarrassment for the navy that a pirate had gotten into Venice so easily.

After months of trying to warn Gio, the doge of Venice, that the pirates needed to be dealt with, he'd finally listened. If one Varangian could get in, that meant many others could too. The fact he was a mage was a whole other mess that was up to Arkon to deal with.

As far as the Republic knew, the Varangians didn't have magic users in their military, apart from their much beloved Wolf Mage. The Varangian emperor openly spoke against magic and persecuted his own people that were found wielding it.

Nico could sense when there was blood in the water, and the Republic's safety was starting to fray about the edges.

Focus on your own fight. Let Arkon and Zahir worry about the Varangians, Nico scolded himself.

The pirates needed to be dealt with *now*, especially because they were no longer harassing the occasional merchant. They were war profiteering, and Nico couldn't abide a traitor. He'd devoted his entire life to Venice, and to see how some pirate was putting his people at risk for money was like sand grating against his skin.

Savio, his first lieutenant, moved up beside him. He was a good-natured sea serpent who gave excellent advice and often was the one to cool Nico's temper when it got out of hand.

"Fine weather for sailing, commander," Savio commented, looking out at the clear blue sky. "We are lucky that the doge gave us the go-ahead to hunt before the fall storms decide to cause trouble."

Nico nodded, not taking his eyes off the horizon. He was impatient, his beast clawing under his skin, desperate to be free.

"Any more news?" he asked.

"Since the raven from Arkon reported that the pirates were seen near the coast of Pag? No. That's their last sighting. I know you don't listen to rumors, but the pirates apparently get a lot of their supplies from Novalja," Savio replied, his dark eyes scanning the deck before going to Nico's face. "Should I be worried about that gleam in your eye? I've known you since we were boys, and it's never led to anything good."

"My beast is restless, that's all. It's distracting me. How long do you think it will take us to get to Pag?" Nico asked.

"The day at least. I don't think going into those waters in the dark is a good idea. It's their territory, not ours."

Nico's teeth ground together. "No. It's the Republic's waters, and I refuse to be afraid of them."

"I'll tell the mages to hurry us along then, shall I?" Savio didn't argue with him, he knew better when Nico was in such a shitty mood. He just gave him a small smile and continued his rounds to make sure the ship was running smoothly.

Nico went back into his cabin and stared at the map of the islands spread out over his small dining table. The islands dotted the Croatian coast like confetti. They had been the home of pirates for as long as history was recorded. If the war front wasn't slowly creeping to the coast, maybe it wouldn't be such an issue.

Technically, the Republic still had the coastline, but smugglers and pirates knew the waters better than anyone in the navy. They could sell and steal from both the Republic and the Varangians, making money off both before retiring to their hideouts and strongholds.

Nico didn't want to go into a fight against their own people. Maybe he would be lenient if they gave over their king to him. One neck for the noose instead of hundreds. They hadn't bothered their own people and had steered well clear of the navy before the damn Pirate King came into the scene. They had made it personal. He didn't have many friends, but Ezra and Zahir were counted among them. To use Nico's personal flag to hurt them... Claws burst through Nico's fingers before he could stop it.

"Enough. Breathe. Breathe. Breathe," he whispered. He hadn't lost control in years, but with each passing day, he felt he was wound tighter and tighter. God help whoever was close by when he finally exploded.

* * *

THE SUN WAS SETTING by the time they sailed through the still waters between the islands and the mainland.

In the days to come, Nico would often regret running his mages ragged in an effort to reach the islands the same day as leaving port. If he hadn't been so pigheaded and agitated, he would've made better decisions.

The mages were close to exhaustion, swaying on their feet and ready to drop. It was why they didn't sense the illusion magic until it was too late. They had sailed the ship in between a merchant galley and the island.

It was a small vessel that barely registered next to the big warship. Nico wasn't ready for the huge chains that lifted from the water. The hull of his ship crashed into them. He was flying out of his chair and was on his feet and running before anyone had a chance to raise the alarm.

"Rowers! To your position! Reverse the ship," Nico shouted, the men already scurrying. He could sense the trap, and when the second chain lifted behind them, the ship was pinned.

Savio was calling for weapons, sending the gunners to the cannons to prepare for whatever came next. The illusion melted off the merchant vessel to reveal a warship flying a black flag.

Nico stripped off his jacket, ready to dive into the water, but he hesitated. The pirates weren't attacking him. They were just...waiting. Nico had rules about not firing on ships that weren't attacking him. No, this was about something else.

That something else soon appeared.

A woman strode across the deck, her red hair blowing like blood in the breeze. She wore black knee-high boots, well-cut black pants, and a dark red shirt with a black vest that accentuated the shape of her hips. She had a blade on her hip and at least three daggers that Nico could spot from the small stretch of water separating them.

"Nicolo D'Argento," she called in a teasing voice, "I thought you would be taller."

The hair on the back of Nico's neck stood up. There was something familiar and knowing in her tone that made him curious and uneasy at the same time.

"You have me at a disadvantage, my lady," he said, his voice carrying across the water. "Who are you meant to be?"

"Sophia Osara, but you might know me by my other title." The woman smiled. It was violence and beauty combined—the divinely terrifying embodiment of feminine rage. "The Pirate King."

CHAPTER TWO

N ico blinked, momentarily too stunned to form words. He opened his mouth and closed it. "Savio, did that woman just say she's meant to be the Pirate King?"

"Yes, commander."

Nico burst out laughing. He couldn't help it. Sophia laughed with him, pulled out a gun, and shot a magical net out at him. Nico was yanked, struggling and swearing, from the deck of the boat before Savio or his crew could grab him. He tried clawing his way through the net, but the magic was too strong, and he hit the deck of the pirate ship with a thud.

Sophia's boots appeared in front of him. The net was removed only to be replaced by magic-nulling cuffs to stop him from shifting.

"Not laughing now, are you?" she said, the tip of her sword placed to his throat. "Tell your men to stand down, or I'll paint my deck with your guts."

Nico got to his feet and signaled to Savio. "Don't fire. I do believe this is a hostage situation?"

"Sure," Sophia replied, her smile too sweet. Up close she was rather cute with a spray of freckles across her tanned face.

How in all the gods did this woman become the Pirate King? Nico was still struggling to believe it.

Savio's face was red as he shouted across the water. "*Signora*, please return the commander, and we shall pay a ransom for him or..."

"Enough. Hobble them," Sophia commanded and signaled to a beefy man at the front of the ship.

Nico tried to shout a warning, but someone clamped a dirty hand over his mouth. Unknown magic rolled hot over the deck before it hit the water and punched hard into the hull of the *Reitia*. Alarms sounded as the crew hurried across the deck to fix whatever damage the mage had suddenly caused.

"Quartermaster? Put him in the brig. First class for the little prince," Sophia commanded.

"Yes, sir," a big man replied with a deep Greek accent. He was almost as tall as Nico with a scar that ran ragged down one side of his face.

Nico was dragged down into the fetid darkness below decks. Savio would be okay. He trusted his first lieutenant to get the ship and crew under control and come after them.

The pirate ship shuddered under Nico's feet, and he knew they were pulling away and fast. His eyes grew used to the darkness, and a heavy hand shoved him forward, down another set of wooden stairs to holding cells.

"First class, like the king requested," the quartermaster said, locking the door behind him.

Nico tried to breathe and think through the red clouding his vision. He had to keep his temper in check and get the hell out of there alive. If only so his aunt didn't kick his ass for being captured so easily.

Not to mention what Arkon, Dom, and Zahir would be like when they found out. He could hear their laughter already. Arkon was always chastising him about thinking too black and white and for underestimating magic. Usually that happened when the sorcerer was cheating at cards.

As a member of the Council of Ten, Nico knew *theoretically* he was a prime target for would-be kidnappers to try and get a ransom. The so-called Pirate King was the first one dumb enough to try it.

Nico paced about the cell and tried to find something that would help him pick the locks on his manacles. They were well made, with glyphs engraved into them to stop any magic the prisoner might have. How did lousy pirates get their hands on such equipment? They must've stolen them from someone used to traveling with rogue *stregoni*. Fuck. This had gotten far more complicated than he had prepared for.

The cell had nothing but a bucket for prisoners to piss in and the wooden boards of the ship. Fixed in the side of the hull, a little higher than his head, was an iron latch that a chain could be put through to lash two prisoners together. The padlock holding it together was shut, so he could even use it as a weapon the next time someone got too close.

Nico prowled up and down the cell. He knew they were heading south and fast, but that was all he knew.

Savio will get the boat fixed and come after you, he repeated.

If the pirates wanted to ransom him out to the Republic, they were going in the wrong direction. They would be better off heading back towards the city. Maybe the captain had other plans.

The fucking Pirate King was a woman. When Nico got back to Venice, he was going to chew Arkon out for not being able to glean that from all the rumors. So much for his fucking ravens being the most effective spies in the Republic.

There was something else that was bothering Nico about his captor. *Osara*. It was a name he was sure he'd heard before. There was a familiarity in it that niggled him. He would have to ask her the next time she held a sword to his throat.

His serpent shifted inside of him, waking up and paying attention. It was the first time in months that the itching under Nico's skin had disappeared. The beast was content. Why, Nico had no fucking idea.

Maybe because it knew its prey was close by. It didn't seem to be bothered by the cuffs that kept him locked in or that they were trapped in a cell.

Osara. The name was like an annoying cut on the inside of his mouth. Did he do his cadetship with an Osara? It seemed likely. It was a Venetian name, and the quickest way to get employment in the Republic was to join the navy. Nico had started at the bottom like everyone else. His father had insisted on it. Like he had insisted on Nico being the best at everything. If he wasn't, there were consequences. A young shifter could regenerate broken bones overnight—this fact Nico had learned more than once.

Don't think of that fucking prick right now. He's dead and you're not. You have to figure out how to get out of this so you can get your hands around the pretty neck of the Pirate King. The serpent rumbled in agreement at the picture Nico was painting.

Well, it was good to know it was on his side for something. He needed to get the cuffs off, and then he could rip through the ship like a child smashing a toy. It was no match for his serpent form. There weren't many ships that were.

The Varangians feared the serpents and were wise to do so. They had also quickly started to develop weapons to use against them. Huge harpoons that could winch them in the air and other projectiles were the only way to kill them. The serpents could move so quickly that only the best marksman had a chance of hitting them.

No one had ever been good enough to hit Nico.

* * *

NICO DIDN'T HAVE TOO much time to wonder about his current fate. Two pirates came down into the brig and opened the doors.

"Captain wants a word," one said, and Nico got to his feet.

"You know, I could make you both very rich men if you let me go," he said casually.

The pirates both laughed at him. "I fear the captain more than I'd want the gold you could give me. I watched her hang and gut a man once. She just stood there and smiled as he screamed. Never saw anything like it."

Nico's serpent thought the man had probably deserved it. Up on deck, the sky was a riot of stars. Lamps had been lit all over the deck. The Pirate King walked down a set of stairs that led to the ship's wheel. The quartermaster was with her, and he didn't look happy.

Interesting.

Sophia put her hands on her hips and stared at him. "I've been thinking, Komēs, that you would look good hanging from my mast."

"Really? The Republic won't pay for a dead man," Nico replied, trying to keep his temper in check. She was rolling out his official title with the ease of someone who knew the navy hierarchies. Definitely from a naval family.

There was an arrogant gleam in her green eyes, a curl of violence to her lips. He really wanted to know if she was any good with the saber she wore at her hip.

"Won't they? There are some things in life worth more than gold," Sophia replied. Nico glanced about her men. More than one of them were sharing angry, pointed looks with the quartermaster.

"Maybe that's just your opinion, Sophia. I wonder if your crew feels the same." Nico looked at the faces around him. They were lean, like they hadn't been eating very well. They also looked tired. Considering the chaos the king had been causing of late, Nico wasn't surprised. "If you hostage me back to the Republic, I will personally ensure that each man is given their body weight in gold."

A murmur ran around the assembled crew like wildfire. Nico tried not to smile. They were pirates after all. They were loyal as long as their captain had their best interests at heart.

"Stop lying to them," Sophia snapped. "You can't ensure shit right now."

"Get me to a Republic trading post, and I can make my claim legal in less than a day," Nico replied. He was still wearing his seal ring, and that was identification enough. Sophia drew a dagger and pressed the tip to his heart. "I don't believe a damn word you say."

"Isn't this the whole point of this game we've been playing? So you can capture me and make money?"

Sophia's eyes narrowed. "No, darling. It's so I have the pleasure of watching the light fade from your eyes."

"That's not what you told us, captain," a voice said from the back of the crowd. "You said we would make a year's wage off his posh ass."

"Plans change. I want to see him die," Sophia said.

Nico's serpent senses could taste blood in the air again. "I don't change my plans. If you all ransom me at the nearest naval outpost, I will ensure you can all retire rich men by the end of the month with no repercussions from the navy."

He looked at the quartermaster standing behind Sophia. His dark eyes were considering the deal, so Nico decided to sweeten it.

"If you ransom me *and* the Pirate King, I will double the price. You don't all need to hang. Just one of you. You should make it her."

"Why, you fucking—" Sophia lunged at him with her dagger, but the quartermaster was faster. He grabbed her from behind and disarmed her. "Kyrios! What the actual fuck? I am your captain and your king!"

"And they made me quartermaster to look out for them, Sophia. Killing the prince is the last fucking straw," he growled and cuffed her in another set of manacles.

CHAPTER THREE

Sophia could not believe her day of victory was getting ruined. She was going to fucking kill Kyrios when she got free of those damn fucking manacles.

Both Sophia and Nico were taken back to the brig, and she was so angry, she couldn't speak. Kyrios attached a chain to Nico's manacles, then to hers, before locking them above their heads through the iron loop.

"Now, you can kick the shit out of each other if you like, but I'm not wasting the med-mage on either of you. Play nice," Kyrios said and smiled. "Or don't, but it's up to you."

"Don't do this, or you will regret it," Sophia promised.

"We have followed you on your vendetta for fucking months without complaint because you promised us the score of a life-time. You would've taken that away from the men just for a chance to kill this piece of shit," Kyrios said, his smile vanishing. "You brought this on yourself, and you know it."

Sophia ground her teeth together and said nothing. Kyrios locked the doors and glanced at Nico.

"You drive a good bargain, prince. I wonder if the

Varangians' offer will double my money. I suppose we will find out," he said before disappearing back up on the deck.

"Well, I suppose while we are hanging here together, you can tell me what I did to piss you off so much?" Nico asked, the chains holding their arms above their arms forced them to stand far too close.

Sophia glared up at his stupidly handsome face. There was no doubt about it. He was a gorgeous serpent with an aquiline nose, long sun-streaked hair, and a fuck you glint in his blue eyes. It was a shame he was such a fucking prick.

"You being a commander in the navy isn't enough?" she replied. She yanked on the chain hard, forcing his arms to jerk. It was petty and stupid, but it made her feel better. She used the slack to try and reach her hair pin.

Kyrios was smart enough to clear out her pockets for daggers and other weapons. Being a dumbass man meant he hadn't considered what she could hide in her thick braid. Her fingers brushed the top of her hair, but she couldn't reach the pin. *Fuck this fucking night.*

"I've got a score to settle with you, sea rat," Nico said. There was something in his voice that made her still.

"And what's that, prince?"

"You let a Varangian mage into my city," he replied.

Sophia, who never knew when to back down from a fight, lifted her chin. "Yeah, I did, didn't I? I got in using your family flag too. Must be nice to just have customs wave all your docking fees and taxes for you every time you enter the city."

Nico's nostrils flared as he crowded her. "That mage hurt two of my friends. Stealing the inventor and his daughter, that I could forgive. It's war after all. But almost getting Zahir and Ezra kidnapped? You made it personal, and I won't forget it."

"Good. I hope it eats away at you, and you dream about me smiling over your dead corpse."

Nico growled, a deeply animalistic sound that reminded her of the water dragon that lived under his perfect skin.

The memory of seeing a serpent in its real form had given Sophia nightmares when she was a child. She might hate the Republic, but she was glad she wasn't a part of the Varangian Navy.

Nico was rumored to be the most vicious of them all. Seeing the coiled ball of violence in front of her in human form, Sophia could believe the rumors. Her brother, Tito, had always said he was the best fighter he'd ever seen.

Don't forget Tito is the reason Nico needs to die. Like Sophia ever forgot that. She pulled on the chain again, making Nico grunt in annoyance, and made another swipe for her braid.

"What on earth are you doing? Apart from trying to piss me off?" Nico asked as his chest bumped into her.

Sophia shut her eyes and let out a tight breath. "Look, just so we are clear, as soon as I'm free, I'm probably going to try and kill you."

"I'm sensing a 'but'."

"There is one if you would stop interrupting me." Sophia wriggled so her back was to him. "There is a bronze hair pin in the top of my braid. Can you reach it with your teeth?"

"And why would I try and do that?"

Sophia moved again to face him. "Are you as thick as you look? If Kyrios really is about to try and deal with the Varangians, there's going to be no happy ending for either of us. The Republic would happily pay a ransom for you, and you'd be back on your ship in no time. If you are sold to the Varangians, they are going to hang you up like you are the goddamn catch of the day. If their torturers push you to the point of shifting, they will take you apart bit by bit and sell every scale, bone, tooth, and drop of blood."

Nico's brows bunched together. "Why would they want any of that?"

"Are you dense? For your magic."

"But the Varangians hate magic."

Sophia prayed for mercy. "You really don't know how the world works, do you, prince? The Varangian political line might allege that they hate magic, but that doesn't mean people aren't doing it. You are a magical creature. They will sell off every part of you for magical cures. There isn't a Varangian sailor in their whole navy who wouldn't want a serpent scale to use as a talisman because they think it will protect them against you."

Nico's confusion turned to anger. "We need to get out of here."

"No shit. Now, try and get the pin out of my hair," Sophia said and turned. Nico's hard body pressed up against her.

"You're too short for me to reach."

"Pull on the chain then," she snapped, her fingers wrapping about the manacles. "Do it."

"It will hurt you."

"Only a little. Why do you care? I made good money off smuggling that mage in, remember?" she goaded him. The fact she had given it to the San Gerolamo Orphanage in Castello that looked after the children whose parents were lost at sea was neither here nor there.

It was enough to piss off the prince because the chain yanked her hard enough to lift her clear off the ground. His face buried in her hair.

"Stop wriggling," he complained.

"I can't help it," she said.

"Got it," he replied through gritted teeth and lowered her back to her feet. Sophia turned, and Nico had the long pin in his perfect teeth.

"Don't drop it or we are fucked." Sophia realized there was only one way she was going to reach the padlock, and she didn't like it.

"Now what?" he asked.

AMY KUIVALAINEN

"Now, I hope your thighs are as strong as they look. I'm going to use my mouth to take the pin, and then I'm going to climb you like a tree to get to the main lock." Nico was giving her an incredulous look. "I don't like it either, but we need to get the chain down. Once it is down, I can pick the manacles."

Nico nodded and didn't try to say anything. Excellent. Peace and quiet at last. Sophia stood up on tiptoes. "Kiss me, big boy."

Nico rolled his eyes and leaned down so her lips could reach his. She tried not to think whose mouth was brushing against hers as he transferred the pin to her mouth. Okay, so she could admit those lips were the softest part about him.

"Yank," she said, gripping the pin tight in her teeth. Nico pulled down on the chain, lifting her up off the ground. She wrapped her legs around his chest as high as she could and held on. That a man could smell so good after being at sea was just another reason to resent him.

Sophia grabbed the chain above his head and used it to haul herself higher and get a leg over one of his shoulders.

"Well, this isn't how I thought my day was going to go," Nico said, looking up at her from between her thighs.

Sophia rolled her eyes at him. She had enough slack in the chain to be able to grab the pin from her mouth and get her grip on it.

"Don't flatter yourself, prince. My pussy would eat you alive," she said and put the pin into the padlock. "Try and hold still so I don't fall."

Nico chuckled, making her wriggle a little. "Sorry. The absurdity of the moment is getting to me."

Sophia tried not to grin. "I've been in worse scrapes. Now, hold still and witness how a master does it."

Nico looked up at her, his face way to close to her crotch. "What? I'm looking as you told me to."

"I changed my mind. Look the other way," she said and got to work, picking the lock.

She had to get out of there so she could gut Kyrios and whoever else thought it was a good idea to fuck with her. Then she would sell Nico back to the Varangians and keep all the money for herself. She wouldn't sail with a bunch of mutineers. Fuck those guys. The padlock popped, and she unlatched the chain.

"Ha!" she said and then swore as she wobbled. Nico caught her before she ate the deck. "Woah. Thanks. No, no thanks. Fuck you." Sophia shoved him away from her. They were still bound by the chain, but at least she could get some space from him and his salt and spice smell.

"Now what, genius? We are on a ship with a whole crew that wants to kill us," Nico asked.

"I want to kill you too," she reminded him and tried to wriggle the pin into her own manacles. She dropped it and swore.

"How about you do my manacles first, and then I can do yours?" Nico suggested.

Sophia laughed. "Yeah, sure. I'll unlock my prisoner so he can kill me."

"I don't need the cuffs off to kill you, sea rat." Nico's smile was pure predator. "I just don't want to have to drag your corpse around with me."

"How about you stop irritating me while I'm working?" Sophia muttered and wriggled her cuffs to try and get the pin back into them.

"*Gesù Cristo*, this is actually painful to watch," Nico said.

"You know what? Why don't you just shut—" Sophia said before she froze.

Something wasn't... Nico tackled her to the deck. Planks exploded right where she had been standing. The sea rushed in before sucking them back out into the dark abyss.

CHAPTER FOUR

Nico floated weightless in the sea, his serpent wanting to get out. He tried to swim and realized he was still attached to Sophia.

Nico pulled her body to him and kicked his way to the surface. He could see clearly in the water, which was why he immediately recognized the shape of the ship that was firing on the pirates. Fucking Varangians.

He needed to get away from them and fast. The stupid bloody manacles around his wrists prevented him from shifting and being remotely useful in a fight. He pulled Sophia to him, making sure her head was out of the water, and gave her a little shake.

"Hey? Are you with me, sea rat?" he asked. She didn't reply. He could feel her rapid heartbeat under his hand. Still alive but knocked out. He momentarily thought about releasing her and letting her drown. The creature inside of him lashed at his insides.

I wasn't really going to do it. I'd have to drag her corpse around anyway, he grumbled back at it.

It had been one of the longest and weirdest nights of his

life. Sophia was a tempest of a woman that was likely to get them both killed, if a stray cannon ball didn't get them first. Nico swam to a piece of floating debris and hauled Sophia onto it.

He needed to get them away from the Varangians. They were distracted, fighting the pirates, and hopefully, no one had keen enough eyesight to see them in the darkness.

Nico made sure Sophia was still breathing before he started kicking. They had to be close to some land. The ship had headed south, sticking to the archipelago of islands. But they had been using magic to boost the sails, so gods knew where they were.

Nico would know where they were when the sun rose; he usually did. For the moment, he only had to go in the opposite direction of where the Varangians were, and everything would be fine.

* * *

NICO WOKE to his face on the wet sand and Sophia standing over him with a large rock in her hands.

"And what do you think you were going to do with that, sea rat?" he asked. She didn't look remotely guilty at being caught out moments before bashing his head in with a rock. "If you kill me, you're still stuck to me."

"I was going to use the rock to try and break the chain, not your pretty face, prince," she grumbled.

Nico smiled and sat up. "You know I don't believe that."

"What happened? Where are we?" Sophia said, staring about at the white sandy beach they were sitting on.

"The Varangians and your crew decided to fight, and while they were busy killing each other, I swam us out of there. You were too busy sleeping," Nico replied.

Sophia unraveled her salty, damp braid and tried getting

some of the sand off her clothes. "I'm surprised you didn't let me drown."

"I'm waiting until I can change in my serpent form, and then I'll eat you in one mouthful."

Sophia's eyes gleamed with sudden humor. "Sounds very kinky of you, prince."

"That's not what I meant," he growled, getting to his feet.

"Don't worry. We all know you are a virgin," Sophia replied and turned back to the tree line. "We need to head in that direction."

"What makes you think that?"

"Because there're some great bushes over there, and I need to pee," she said, tugging on the chain to get him moving. "I have sand in places where there should not be sand and have lost a ship and a crew, so get moving. I'm in no mood to put up with a man's bullshit this morning."

"I'm surprised you care about a crew that turned on you," he replied.

"They only did that because you wouldn't keep your mouth shut." Sophia stomped up the beach, her hair like a beacon in the morning sun. Nico had the sudden urge to run his fingers through it.

"Those Varangians turned up out of nowhere. I didn't hear any of the alarms go off up on deck. Did you?" she asked.

"No, nothing. Perhaps they were using the new technology that the inventor was creating. You know, the inventor you sold to them." Nico had been wondering about how the ship had been able to get the jump on them too.

"Maybe. It serves Kyrios right for being such a shithead and trying to sell me to them. Men!" Sophia kicked a piece of driftwood. The chain was long enough that when she went behind a bush, Nico thankfully didn't have to follow. He turned his back to be polite.

"Do you have a plan, prince?" she asked when she re-emerged.

"Find out where we have landed and go from there," Nico replied. "The Republic owns the coast for now, so we are bound to find someone that can help us."

Sophia bundled her tangled hair into a knot. "Hopefully they can help us with breakfast too. I'm starving."

"You do realize you're my captive now?" Nico pointed out.

"So? That doesn't mean I'm not starving. If you wanted me dead, you would've let me drown," Sophia said. She shrugged. "I figure you want something."

"I want to find someone who can get these manacles off, and then I'll decide what to do with you, sea rat," he replied.

Nico had a lot of questions, starting from where she had dropped off the inventor to who her family was and how come she managed to smell like roses after being half drowned the night before. He shook that last thought away. It was just his serpent being unpredictable again.

Nico remembered what she had said about the Varangians doing magic and harvesting magical creatures. Arkon would need to talk to Sophia about that too.

For the time being, he had to keep them both alive, which meant he really needed to find out where they were.

He lifted his nose in the air and breathed in deeply. He filtered out the smell of Sophia's perfume and tried to focus.

"Are you...scenting the air right now?" she asked.

"Yes, now be quiet so I can focus." Nico's nose was hypersensitive in his human form. He caught the scents of wild olive and cypress trees and then the briefest hint of cooking fires. "We head that way."

Sophia gave him a cocky salute, and he fought the urge to sigh.

"How about while we walk, you tell me why you thought it was a good idea to sell the inventor to our enemies?" he asked.

"You mean your enemies."

"You're Venetian."

"So?"

"You have no loyalty to your Republic?" Nico pressed as they cleared the trees. There was a small path, and he could smell people had used it recently.

"The Republic never had any loyalty to me, so why should I fucking care?" Sophia said, trailing behind him. "We weren't all raised as pampered little princes."

"You don't know shit about me, woman," Nico growled, his temper flaring.

"The fuck I don't. I knew enough growing up on the docks and seeing my brother and everyone else of lower class never getting promoted over the rich kids in the navy," she snarled back. She yanked on the chain. "You know what? Fuck you. I don't owe you or the Republic fucking shit. It was this stupid war that killed my brother and ruined my family."

"And this is why you hate me so much? Because you have some grudge against Venice?" Nico demanded.

"No. I fucking hate you because you got promoted over my brother. He deserved to be a commander, and they gave it to you, the snotty serpent prince! The next time he sailed out with your fucking father, he died. So fuck you and fuck fucking Venice!" she shouted.

"God, you got a mouth on you." Nico kept walking. He couldn't remember her brother at all, even if the name Osara rang a bell. If he had sailed under Nico's father, then they definitely would have come up through the ranks together. His father liked to keep an eye on his son to ensure that he wasn't being a disappointment.

"Killing me will just make everything easier for the Varangians, especially because you handed them the one man that could change the war in their favor. We've owned the seas, and now you have fucked that for everyone," Nico said, pulling her along. He was mad again, and he hated being reminded of his father at any time.

"Council of Ten, the Varangians, it doesn't matter. No one gives a shit about the little people," Sophia said. "I know that for a fact. I've been an orphan in that city, and it's because of you. That's why I've sworn to take you down. I don't give a shit about the Republic because it never gave a shit about me."

Nico whirled on her. "You say that now, but when the Varangians invade, there will be even more orphans like you in Venice. Maybe you will get one of them swearing revenge on you like you swore revenge on me. Or maybe not, because if they have a drop of magic, the Varangians will just kill them for existing. I hope your revenge is fucking worth it."

Sophia sucked in a breath, her face turning red. Before she could detonate, an old man leading a donkey came down the track towards them.

Thank Reitia for small mercies. Nico smiled and lifted a hand in greeting. He needed to separate himself from the woman by his side before he really did wring her selfish neck. The information she could give them be damned.

CHAPTER FIVE

Sophia was still too angry to even look in Nico's direction for too long. Damn stupid serpent. The old man they encountered informed them they had landed on Corfu. Nico had gotten directions to the nearest village with a smile of relief. Sophia didn't feel even a little bit relieved. Corfu was great, just not for a prisoner.

Kyrios must've really been pushing the mages to get so far, Sophia thought. It didn't surprise her. He was a good enough quarter-master but didn't have the foresight to be a good captain. She wondered if any of the crew had survived.

Serve them right for being a bunch of good for nothing mutineers. She did lament the loss of her ship, but maybe she had a better one in her future. A future she could no longer tell because her favorite tarot deck had also gone down with the ship.

Fucking Kyrios. He'd better be dead before she caught up with him.

Sophia walked in stubborn silence to Benitses, a small beachside village, and continued to remain silent when Nico bartered for a horse. He flashed his signet ring and told them they could come and get the horse from the fortress as well as a bag of gold. Only a rich boy would offer a whole bag of gold for the borrow of one horse.

Nico turned to her. "Are you going to be difficult if I pick you up and put you on the horse first?" Sophia shrugged and said nothing. "Taking that as a yes."

She was going to force all her body weight down and...and it made no difference because his muscles weren't for show. He grabbed her by the hips and lifted her onto the nag without a bat of his long eyelashes. Fucking shifters.

Nico mounted behind, took the reins, and they were on their way. Sophia wobbled and thought about the merits of purposely falling off just to take him down with her. She decided that while it would be amusing, it could backfire, and she could end up breaking a bone or more if he landed on her.

Sophia tried to lean forward a little so her ass wasn't rubbing against him, but that only made her more unsteady. She tried not to think about what he said about her making orphans. It hadn't occurred to her when she was trading the inventor and his daughter for her ship.

The Republic would never be lost to Varangia just because they suddenly had ships that could move quickly. Venice had too many magic users that would destroy any chances of Varangia getting close.

They would blow up the only bridge to the mainland to keep them from coming from land, and as soon as one of their boats entered the lagoon, the sea serpents would destroy it. Not all of them were a part of the Navy. There were always those that stayed in Venice and would rise up to protect her if needed.

Nico was just being dramatic to make her feel bad. She *hated* that it was working. It made her feel worse that she'd lost her ship that was the price of the inventor.

Kyrios *better* be lying at the bottom of the sea, or Sophia would hunt him worse than she'd ever hunted Nico.

Because revenge has worked out so well for you, sorella mia, Tito's voice whispered to her. She still missed him every day.

What would he think of all this? Sophia knew he would be furious that she could be so reckless and stupid to try and take on the D'Argentos.

Nico's father, Lucio, had gone down in the same naval battle that Tito had been in. Lucky for him because he was the one that Sophia would've really liked to kill.

Tito had been up for promotion that would have ensured that their mother and Sophia would finally have to stop worrying about where the money would be coming from.

Tito had gotten a position on Lucio's boat, but Nico had gotten to be commander. It was the biggest load of shit Sophia had ever seen, and she'd seen a lot. Then Tito had died, followed swiftly by her mother because try as she might, Sophia couldn't get the money for her treatments. She caught pneumonia the first winter after Tito's death, and then Sophia was all alone. Alone and plotting.

Tito was the kindest person Sophia had ever seen. He didn't resent Nico getting his job. He had simply shrugged and said, 'Better luck next time.' There had been no next time.

Sophia spiraled down into her memories, barely noticing the pretty landscape or the odd looks they got every time they met someone on the road. She had stopped in Corfu more than once when she and the men needed to get supplies or blow off steam.

A new thought occurred to her. If she could get away, she knew Bettina at the dock whorehouse would hide her. She knew Sophia was good for the credit. At least, until everyone found out she'd lost her fucking ship.

Surely, Nico would take the damn manacles off once they got to the fortress. Sophia would get her chance; she only had to wait. Cheered by the plan, Sophia thought about all the wine she was going to drink to forget about the nightmare that had been trying to capture Nico D'Argento.

There had always been a fortress in Corfu, but its Venetian additions had been built on Byzantine foundations in the early fifteenth century. After magic had returned and the world had collapsed, Venice had reclaimed the fortress as an outpost for the Navy.

Now, it had been completely rebuilt and had taken back the old name of Castel a Mare, the Castle by the Sea. Once, Sophia had to bail out Kyrios from the dungeons after a wild night went sideways. The guards were expensive to bribe, and she didn't have a *soldo* to her name.

"Ah, my new accommodations. I wonder how much will be left of me by tomorrow morning," she said, finally breaking her silence.

"Well, that silence lasted a whole two hours. Longer than I thought you would," Nico replied.

Was that humor in his voice? Sophia doubted it. He looked about as funny as a heart attack.

"I don't see you coming to hang out in a cell with me, so at least I'll get this chain off," Sophia continued aloud. "I don't suppose I could convince you to hand me a dagger or something?"

"And risk you putting it in my back? Not likely," he replied, his breath tickling the back of her neck.

"I'd definitely stab you in the front, so you'd know that it was me," she said.

They stopped at the tall wrought iron gates, and Nico helped her down.

"My name is Commander Nicolo D'Argento. I need an audience with Governor Rafail Ganotis and a phone," he told the guards, showing him his ring. The guard nodded and opened the gate for them.

Just like that. No argument. Not even a blink. Sophia was starting to think she should have stolen the ring when she had the chance.

The governor joined them before they'd even made it to the main doors of the compound. He was a rotund man with a wide smile for the commander.

"Nico, my boy! What has happened?" He looked at Sophia, bushy brows inching higher up his forehead. "Is this a sex thing gone wrong?"

"Christ, no." Nico laughed in a way that showed his perfect teeth, and Sophia tried not to feel offended. He'd be *lucky* to spend a night with her. It would be the best damn night of his life. Nico ignored her glare. "I took custody of this woman right before I had an encounter with the Varangians. I'm going to need a secure room to hold her in. She has important intel for Arkon, and I can't risk anything happening to her."

He hadn't mentioned she was a pirate which was smart of him. If he had, Sophia was sure Rafail would've had a noose around her neck, and she would be hanging from one of the garden's pretty cypress trees in no time.

"I'll see what we can organize that will serve as a cell in the main house. You, commander, will be my honored guest. Anything in my power, you name it, and it's yours," Rafail said, smiling widely.

Nico lifted the chain. "I think we should start with the blacksmith."

CHAPTER SIX

Nico couldn't remember the last time he was so grateful to have a bath and access to fresh clothes. His wrists had red marks around them and felt strangely light now that he wasn't attached to the hellion.

Sophia had been locked into a room that was practically a comfortable cell with a small window. There were guards patrolling the grounds at all times as well as two stationed outside of her door.

Sophia didn't strike him as the type of woman to be afraid of anything, but he'd picked up the scent of fear coming from her when talking about going into the cells under the fortress.

Nico's serpent had scratched his insides to pieces over the thought of anyone hurting her. It made no sense because from what he knew of Sophia, she would make friends with every criminal in there, and they would have a riot on their hands before dawn.

She had looked about the little room he'd put her in like she couldn't quite believe he would make sure she was okay. There was a catch. Nico needed the information she had and would make sure she was alive and able to speak when they got back to Venice.

Nico's serpent was free from the magical manacles, but it was still restless. It didn't like having Sophia out of his sight.

Was it a prey thing? He knew from experience how obsessive a serpent could get on the hunt. It usually went away once the person he was hunting was caught or dead.

Nico was still restless, which was why when Rafail had given him a cell phone to use, he'd taken it outside into the gardens. He stood in the shadows of the poplar and cypress trees, Sophia's window in eyesight. It was enough to keep his serpent happy.

Nico had other reasons for wanting to be outside. It wasn't that he didn't like the governor, but he didn't trust the walls not to have ears.

Nico knew better than to try and call Arkon's phone. He liked to use it as a paper weight and rarely charged it. Magic had made phones expensive and unpredictable with their artifice adjustments. Nico didn't have time to send a message by magical means. He needed Arkon to hear what he had to say as soon as possible, so a call had to do.

Nico rang the doge's palace and got one of the staff members to physically take the phone to Arkon. The kitchen staff quickly put together a plate of food for them to carry because unless food was involved, no servant in the palace could find the sorcerer's rooms. Arkon was a prick like that.

Nico stared at the window, the full moon and his shifter abilities making it clear as day. He had a predator's focus on it, so much so that when Arkon grumbled into the phone, Nico had to shake himself to focus again.

"Nico! Are you there?" Arkon demanded, sounding pissed. That was no surprise. The sorcerer only had two modes— teasing or pissy. He was dramatic to a fault.

"I'm here, and I'm about to ruin your day," Nico replied.

"Where are you?"

"Corfu. I washed up here last night," Nico replied.

There was a long silence at the other end of the line.

"Okay, I'm paying attention now. What the fuck is going on?" Arkon asked, his irritation turning to deadly focused. This was the true Arkon, though the only people who really got to see this side of him were his inner circle or the people who had crossed him and were about to die.

Nico told him the whole truth of it, including the embarrassment of the magical netting gun and the unexpected fact that the Pirate King was a woman. Arkon didn't tease him; he would save that for later. When Nico got to the part about Sophia telling him about Varangians harvesting him, Arkon sucked in a breath.

"You need to get her back to Venice. What the fuck kind of people are using pieces of shifters for magic? It must be some kind of soldier folk practice," Arkon said.

"I don't know, but she acted like I was the stupid one for not knowing. She has worked with the Varangians enough that we can use her for information."

"Do you think you can make a deal with her? What is she like?"

Nico thought about it. "Too dangerous and beautiful to live."

"Well, once we get what we need out of her, you can always hang her. The infamous Pirate King finally taken down. I'm sure Gio will give you a medal," Arkon replied.

Nico's serpent really didn't like that. He rubbed at the sudden pain in his chest.

"She's not going to agree to anything if we hang her afterwards. It will have to be a proper deal to save her life and probably line her pockets," Nico replied.

Arkon laughed. "She's not stupid then. Maybe see if you can get her to sweeten the deal for us too while you are negotiating.

She can help us locate the inventor and his daughter. Get them back, and Gio will give you both medals."

Nico looked up to see Sophia squeezing out the tiny slit of a window and looping her feet into the wisteria that climbed the walls.

"I have to go," Nico said.

"Why? I've only just got to the good stuff."

"Because this maniac of a woman is currently trying to climb out of a three-story window and is going to break her neck," Nico replied and laughed. He couldn't help himself. She really was a maniac.

"God, Nico, I don't think I've ever heard you laugh like that before. What's next? A girly giggle? She must be quite something."

"Yeah, she is a pain in my ass. Get ahold of Savio for me and have the ship come and get us. I'll get her into a deal. And Arkon? Find out what you can on her family. I've known an Osara, but I can't place them," Nico replied.

"You could ask her, you know?"

Nico huffed out another laugh. "I don't trust her to tell me the truth." Nico hung up and checked the progress the sea rat was making.

Sophia was already halfway down the wall, climbing like an expert. The vines were nothing next to the rigging that she was used to. Nico crept silently though the trees, and as she was about to hit the ground, he held out a hand to her.

"May I be of assistance?" he asked.

Sophia yelped and toppled backward, Nico catching her before she could hit the ground. She had bathed and changed into fresh clothes and smelled of roses and lavender soap. The serpent purred.

"I can't believe you just stood there and watched me climb all that way," she said, staring up at him accusatorially.

"You were doing so well. I didn't want to break your stride."

Nico put her back on her feet. "Did you really think there was going to be no one guarding you? You must think I'm an idiot."

Sophia pulled a face. "Maybe I just *hoped* you were when you put me in my own room with a window I could squeeze through."

"I told you, you are too valuable a prisoner. It seems that we are going to have to do things the hard way. From now on, you're not leaving my side. I need to get you to Venice, and I'll see it through, even if I have to throw you over my shoulder and carry you there."

Sophia sighed. "You should hang me. Why delay it?"

"Because I've just talked Arkon into letting me offer you a deal for your life. Now, let's go," Nico replied. When she refused to move, he growled in frustration and tossed her over his shoulder.

"Put me down this instant!" she demanded, beating against his back.

"I gave you the chance to come on your own two feet, and you refused. Deal with it, sea rat."

"Hang me already. I'm too tired to deal with this," she complained, her body going limp.

Nico carried her through the fortress, the servants gaping and quickly getting out of the way. Sophia painted the air blue with every step he took, and he had to stop himself from laughing.

Arkon was right. It took a lot for him to laugh about anything, but Sophia's antics had driven him straight through anger and frustration to amusement. Nico didn't put her down until they got back to his rooms.

"The governor had some very interesting equipment in his weapons vault. One of them was this," Nico said. He took the pair of cuffs from the desk and fixed one around her wrist and then one to his own. The chain spread between them, lengthening and shortening with magic. It allowed about fifteen feet in length before it stopped widening. "Clearly, Corfu has dealt with rogue *stregoni* before. If you had any magic, every time you tried to use it, the cuff would drain you and send your power to me. I can use mine just fine. Incredible work. This great little piece of artifice will also ensure there are no more climbing out of windows."

"Were you born a dick, or is it something you developed in rich boy school?" Sophia asked.

"I wanted to give you the freedom to roam, and you tried escaping again. This is your fault, sea rat." Nico sat down at the small dining table with a sheet of paper and ink. He pointed to the chair beside him. "Please, sit down, Sophia. We are going to do this officially so you should resist trying to kill me in my sleep."

Sophia sat with a resigned sigh. "At least call for wine. It's been a long day."

On that, Nico could agree.

CHAPTER SEVEN

S ophia was starting to think that she had been cursed by the goddess. Was Reitia pissed at her for the inventor thing? Was Fate giving her the finger?

Maybe she should have known better than to think she could escape from a serpent. She'd been given a room with an open window, and she couldn't help herself.

The servants brought food and wine for them both, Nico thanking them without looking up from whatever he was writing. Sophia downed her wine and refilled her glass.

"Are you ready to talk yet?" Nico asked her, finally looking up from his papers.

"About what, Nicolo? The weather we've been having?"

Nico sipped his wine. "This is not the time to hide behind your bullshit. I'm trying to keep Gio from hanging you. You could try and be a little more grateful and meet me halfway. I need to give them something to risk letting you go free."

Freedom. She didn't think that was on the negotiation table at all. Saved from the hangman but imprisoned for all of her days was more than what she had in mind.

"What do you think they would want?" she asked, picking up her knife and fork. She contemplated the knife.

"I wouldn't," Nico said, reading her mind.

"It's too blunt to be of any use. Besides, we are playing nice, aren't we?" Sophia said, batting her lashes at him. She cut into the perfect pan-fried fish on her plate. When was the last time she'd had a decent meal? The last few days had been a blur. Not to mention the last few weeks. She had been almost manic in her efforts to draw Nico out of Venice. Maybe her crew had been right to mutiny against her.

"Do you even know how to play nice?" Nico asked, an amused tick in the corner of his mouth. Did he have to look so good all the time? It was insulting. And distracting.

"I can play very nice if it works in my favor," she replied.

"It is definitely in your favor. Arkon wanted me to bring you home and hang you. You need to give him something."

"Like what? I know lots of things. It comes with the job of being the Pirate King."

Nico ate a mouthful of food. "He's obsessed with the Wolf Mage and any magic that the Varangians might be using. The appearance of a Varangian mage had him irritated, but the possibility of there being more will really give him heartburn."

Sophia thought about it for a while, eating everything on her plate and going back to the platters for more. She had learned long ago that while there was food, you ate as much as you could.

"Varangia is a big empire. There're a lot of superstitious practices that might not look magic but definitely are," she said at last. "I did hear a rumor from a soldier that the Wolf Mage and Emperor Arkadi haven't been seeing eye to eye recently, but I don't know how much truth is in soldiers' talk."

"It's a good start." Nico topped up their wine glasses. "They really want the inventor back."

Sophia almost choked on her mouthful of bread. "That's a big ask considering where they have taken him."

"And where is that?" Nico asked.

Sophia opened her mouth and closed it. "Nice try, but your pretty blue eyes aren't good enough to get that information out of me for free."

"You think my eyes are pretty?" he asked, and she scowled. He had the audacity to actually grin at her. "Okay, Sophia, tell me what you think the information is worth."

She really didn't like the way he said her name with his deep commander's voice. It was all...sexy disapproval.

Sophia stopped thinking about the stupid attraction she seemed to have developed for her enemy and tried to focus on his question. What was the information she had worth? More than just her life and freedom. She had lost everything thanks to Kyrios. She had a few stashes of money in banks around the Mediterranean but not enough to start again.

"I want what you promised my crew. I want my body weight in gold and all the charges against me wiped," she said and drank more wine. He could afford it.

"They won't let you go without some kind of written agreement that you won't turn to piracy again," he said.

"Then I want twice my body weight in gold. You really think I turned to piracy because I had lots of money lying around? If I had enough to set up a new life, I wouldn't be pirating. I can't even go back to it now thanks to the bullshit mutiny you caused."

Nico leaned back in his chair and considered her. His eyes tracked the pattern of the freckles that ran over her cheeks and down her throat. Did his shifter senses pick up how fast her heart was racing? God, she hoped not.

"You are the Pirate King. Can't you just go back to it without the crew?" he asked.

"Not how it works. I was voted in as the king because I have dirt on all the other captains out there. Blackmail got me my seat, and you can't be a king if you don't have a crew. I have all the information on them still, but it's useless."

Nico's smile returned. "Not necessarily. Let's focus on the Varangians first, and then, if you want to extend your offer with information on your fellow pirates, I will let you negotiate with Arkon."

"The raven king himself, huh? Why not you? Don't you have the authority?"

"I do," Nico said and let out a small huff of a laugh. "I just want to see you two across the table from one another. I think you're the only person that might be able to put the little shit in his place."

Sophia's neck went hot at the praise. It was unexpected and unwelcome. "I hear he likes the ladies. Maybe we'll end up falling in love."

"Oh, he'll definitely fall in love with you. He won't be able to help himself."

Nico went back to writing the contract, and Sophia was content to finish eating and drinking her wine. She risked glancing over at him sporadically. She couldn't help it. She'd been around powerful shifters before but never an alpha.

Nico was most definitely an alpha. He had an aura about him that made you want to obey him. Sophia had always had a problem with authority figures, so it was no wonder that they rubbed sparks off each other. She wanted to push him to the point he exploded. She really wanted to see what he looked like angry. It was probably magnificent.

Sophia shelved that idea for another time. They had a deal to make, and she didn't want him changing his mind. She could play nice until she got what she wanted.

Nico wasn't satisfied until the plates had long since been cleared away and Sophia was ready to curl up in a ball and go to sleep. She had taken to walking about the large guest suite to test the length of the magical chain that was now attached to her. It was long enough that she could make it into the bathroom and shut the door behind her. At least she would have some privacy for that, unlike today behind the bush.

She eyed the large king-sized bed covered in linens so white and soft, she was sure she would dirty them just by looking at them for too long. One bed and they were chained together. That was going to be interesting.

When Sophia finally wandered back into the main area, Nico was standing by the window, looking out at the moon, his eyes shining with a shifter gleam. "The contract is on the table. Read it, and if you are happy with it, sign it."

Sophia took up the three-page document and read through it. There was a lot of posh legal speak in it, but it amounted to what she wanted—total freedom with a pardon for her crimes and twice her weight in gold. In return, she would tell them everything she knew about where the inventor had been taken, the Varangian encampments she'd done business with, and all the information pertaining to magic use within the empire.

Sophia read the contract twice, just to make sure she didn't miss anything, before she signed it.

"Here you go, commander," she said, fanning herself with the pages. She had drunk a bit too much wine, so she added cheekily, "Sure you don't want to seal the deal with a kiss and a handshake? That's how pirates do it."

She closed her eyes and pouted up at him. She yelped as he grabbed her by the face and kissed her hard and searing. It was more of a bite than a kiss, his soft lips scorching and gone just as suddenly. He let her go, and she stumbled back, too shocked and dazed to react. He grabbed her hand and shook it.

"There. It's done," he said, his cheeks red. *Sweet goddess of the sea.*

He leaned down until their noses almost touched, his eyes

blue fire. "But just so we are clear, don't even think about trying to seduce me to get this chain off. It won't work."

Sophia raised a red brow. "Oh, sweet boy. If I really wanted to seduce you, you wouldn't stand a chance. But because you brought up boundaries, the left side of the bed is mine."

"How about I take the bed, and you take the floor?" Nico replied.

Sophia looked over at the huge king-sized bed. "How about you take the floor, and I take the middle?"

"Left side it is," Nico said, kicking off his boots.

Sophia hid her smile. The goddesses might not hate her after all.

CHAPTER EIGHT

Nico knew that kissing Sophia was a mistake. She was so irritatingly cocky that when she pouted, he couldn't help himself. The shock on her face had been worth it.

Now, lying beside her in bed, it was coming back to haunt him. Her smell was all over everything, drowning his sensitive senses. It was problematic, just like the rest of her.

His serpent was content, so he hoped he would get some sleep. He rolled over and found Sophia awake and staring at him.

"Thinking about wrapping the chain around my neck and choking me out? Because I don't swing that way," he said sleepily.

"It occurred to me, but you're a bit bigger than me."

"Hasn't stopped you so far." Nico knew that this was about as gentle she got, so he said, "We are allies now, so I want you to know whatever I did to piss you off so much, I'm sorry."

Sophia rolled onto her back and stared at the canopy. "I blamed you, but it was your father I was really mad at. And mine."

"And he's not around anymore to take your revenge out on?"

"I don't know. I have no clue who he is."

Nico knew this was new ground for them. He didn't really know how to 'people' like Arkon did, or how to be charming like Dom.

"Why do you hate him if you don't know who he is?" he asked.

"He is a serpent shifter, and that's all I know. Why do you think I hate you all so much? He was an entitled twat too," Sophia said.

Little warning lights started flashing in Nico's head. She was a serpent? It made some sense with how aggressive she was on the seas and how his own inner beast reacted to her.

Nico needed more information. "Can you shift?"

"Nope. It's why I don't know who my father is." Sophia turned her head to look at him. "You probably don't want to know this, I'm sorry. Go to sleep."

"No, I do. We are allies. Allies tell each other things." Nico cringed inwardly. He sounded like a complete idiot.

Sophia's lips twitched in an almost smile. "If you say so. My mother was a singer. A chorus girl at *La Fenice*. My father was a serpent shifter that she had a passionate love affair with. Like most rich assholes, he promised her the world and delivered on none of it. She got pregnant with my brother, Tito, and me. Our father said that due to who his family was, the only way he could legally claim us was if we both shifted. We were tested when we came of age, and as the doctor said, we were both duds. Our father never claimed us, and it broke my mother. She worked at the theatre until she became too sick. Even on her deathbed, she refused to tell me who the *bastardo* was."

Tito. Now, that name rang a bell. Nico got a flash of red hair and a bright smile. He hadn't thought about him in years. He had been one of the only people who were nice to Nico through their basic training.

"I'm sorry about your father," Nico said, and he suddenly had a new mission for Arkon. "And for your brother. I remember him now. We went through our cadetship together. He was an incredible sailor and soldier. It makes sense that you both have serpent blood. You're formidable on the waters; that's for sure."

"I'm glad I caused you a few headaches," Sophia said.

"More than a few."

Sophia *did* smile at that. "Yeah, Tito would be so mad about it. He really liked you."

"He did?"

"Said that you were the best soldier he'd ever seen. It's one of the reasons he wasn't mad that you got the commander position over him. I was furious because you were just another rich serpent that got a job over someone of lower class," Sophia said and screwed her face up. "Still kind of mad at you to be honest. Tito got a job on your father's ship, and the next time he sailed out, he never sailed back. Tito said that your old man was a great general but a shit father."

Nico flinched. "He *was* a shit father. Can I tell you something that will probably make you madder at me?"

"Is that wise when we are getting along so nicely, exchanging childhood trauma?" Sophia asked.

"Just trying to be honest," Nico replied, and she gave him a nod. "I hated my father. I was relieved when I got the position because it meant I was out from under his command. I worked so hard to get it because I needed to get the fuck away from him. He was so angry when I got that commission, he stabbed me with a stiletto."

Sophia's brows shot up. "You're fucking kidding me."

"No. Shifters...heal quickly. He took advantage of that." Nico's jaw worked, his hatred coming out like old poison. "I'm sorry your brother died, but the day I heard my father was dead on that ship was one of the best days of my life."

Sophia studied his face, like she didn't know whether to be

angry at him or not. It didn't change how he felt about it. His relief had been so potent, he had collapsed on the deck of his ship and cried. Everyone thought it was grief. He let them.

"Shifter families are hard when there are two alphas in the house. It's not just a problem with the poorer ones either. I couldn't escape him or my name. I couldn't leave the house until I got that commission for myself, and he couldn't control me anymore."

"And your mother didn't step in?"

"She wasn't around. She left when I was ten. She couldn't live with him anymore, and she couldn't take me with her," Nico replied. He shouldn't be telling her this. She had openly said that she was good at getting information out of people to bribe them with. It wasn't like it was a secret, not after so long.

"At least my father had the courtesy of staying away from my brother and me. I was always sadder for Mother than I was for not having a father around. Plenty of kids at the docks had no fathers," Sophia said. She frowned playfully. "I suppose I have to stop hating you now that we know each other better."

"It would make life easier," he replied, lifting the chain for her to see. "I can't let you go until you help Arkon."

"I'm not going anywhere until I have my gold," she pointed out. Her green eyes glimmered with mischief. "And I'm going to eat like a starving horse between now and Venice so I'm as heavy as I can possibly be when I get weighed for my reward."

Nico laughed softly. "I would expect nothing less from you, sea rat. You look like you could do with some regular meals anyway."

"I should eat nothing but cake between here and Venice. I have to make it worth my while."

Nico shook his head at her. "Go to sleep. Savio will be here with my ship tomorrow, and we'll have to go back to pretending we hate each other. Shouldn't be too hard. You are very argumentative."

"I can't help it." Sophia lifted one shoulder. "You're fun to fight with."

With that, she rolled over, stole most of the blanket, and went to sleep.

CHAPTER NINE

Nico woke the following morning with a knee in his ribs and an arm slung over his face. It took him a few moments to remember that Sophia was in bed beside him. His dick didn't need the reminder.

Horrified at how hard he was, Nico slipped out from underneath her arm and went to use the bathroom. His eyes were all serpent, a splay of scales rising up over one arm.

What the hell is the matter with you? He splashed his face with cold water, and when that didn't work, he stepped into the shower. The chain around his wrist shone silver in the morning light, reminding him of his duty.

He needed to get back to Venice as soon as possible. He was a creature of routine, and everything had been upside down for days.

Sophia was definitely to blame. Sophia, who was actually of serpent blood. He really needed to talk to Arkon and figure out which highborn serpent had fathered her. Shifter families weren't like normal families. It didn't matter that the father hadn't officially claimed Sophia and Tito; he still had claim on them.

The growl that came out of Nico shook him back to the present moment. He really didn't like anyone having a claim over his prize. It made the serpent want to fight. Not that it was so unusual.

Nico got out of the shower, dressed, and summoned some breakfast. He had to give it to Rafail; he was accommodating. It paid to keep Venice happy and their generals. The servant came in with a breakfast tray and passed him a sealed messaged.

"Note for you, sir. It appeared on the tray," he said.

"Thank you," Nico replied and grinned at Arkon's seal. He opened it, and his smile widened. Savio would be in Corfu with his ship by midday. *Thank Reitia.* He needed some kind of normalcy back in his life, and he was anxious to be on his way.

"You better have ordered enough for two," Sophia said, coming into the room. Her red hair was a wild tangle, and she only wore a men's button-up shirt that hung to her knees. Dear gods, he wasn't mentally ready to deal with that yet. Sophia grabbed a piece of bacon from the tray with her fingers on her way to the chair beside him.

"Damn, I haven't had a sleep like that in months," she said, stretching her arms over her head.

"Your favorite position was a knee in my ribs," Nico commented, plating up some food for her.

Her sleepy smile turned devilish. "That's not my favorite position," she said, waggling her brows as she bit into her bacon.

Nico handed her the plate, hoping she didn't notice the heat creeping up his neck. "Eat up. The *Reitia* will be here soon, and we can get on our way."

Sophia guzzled her coffee like it was the elixir of life. "Do I have time to have a shower? It's a luxury I don't usually get. I'll let you wash my back if you ask nicely."

"Thanks, but I already had my shower," he replied.

Sophia only smirked. Was it the serpent side of her that made her poke at him? Or was it just her?

He wasn't indifferent to how beautiful she was. He idly wondered what he would be missing in the morning if he did take her to bed properly.

No, not thinking about it. She was the worst kind of criminal—one that put the Republic in jeopardy.

Nico didn't think she came up for air once as she wolfed down her food, poured herself more coffee and headed to the shower. He read the paper and tried not to smile at the bawdy tavern songs Sophia decided to sing in the bathroom at the top of her lungs. Arkon was definitely going to fall in love with her.

His serpent scratched at him, and he let out a frustrated sigh. As soon as he got her safely on the deck of his ship, he would take off his cuff and go for a proper swim. The beast was irritating him more than usual, and he had a sneaking suspicion the pirate in the bathtub was to blame.

Nico was starting to think Sophia had drowned when she finally re-emerged. She was glowing with good humor, her hair braided back and dressed in the clothes Rafail had the servants wash for her. Nico wondered if she ever wore a dress and then dismissed the idea immediately. She wasn't a dress kind of girl, and he didn't mind the pants showing off her great ass.

"Thank you for that. I might live at sea, but I have a thing about being clean. My next ship is going to have a proper bathtub," she said.

"The *Reitia* has one," he found himself saying. He cleared his throat. "But we will make sure we get the mages to get the boat moving. Arkon is eager to meet you, and I can't stay cuffed to you forever."

Sophia poked him in the chest. "You say that like you haven't been having the time of your life the past few days. This is probably the most fun a rich boy like you has ever had."

"I think we have different ideas of fun."

"I think *you* just refuse to admit that we don't," Sophia

mimicked and patted his cheek. "Don't worry, *amico mio*. I won't tell anyone."

"We are friends now?" he asked, crossing his arms.

"*Allies* is another word for friends. We shared childhood trauma and shit father stories. That makes us kind of friends." Sophia put her hands on her hips. "Or I could go back to fighting with you. The choice is yours."

"Gods no. Fight with me later once we are back on my ship. I just want to be back on the water," Nico said.

It took another hour to be free of Governor Rafail, who wasn't happy that Nico was cutting his visit early. Nico promised to send him back two casks of his favorite Chianti once he got back to Venice, then they were finally free of him.

Down at the docks, the fishermen were returning with their daily hauls, and the markets were in full swing. They got a few curious looks, but one glare from Nico had them looking away just as quickly. He spotted the *Reitia*, and the tightness in his chest eased. The hull looked okay from whatever the pirate mage had done to it. Savio was waiting by the gang plank.

"Commander, nice to see you in one piece," he said, his eyes glancing to Sophia. She was looking at a well-dressed woman out shopping.

"Alive and well. This is the Pirate King—" Nico began, but Sophia tapped on his arm.

"Give me some money. I have an idea," she said.

Savio's brows shot up.

"I don't have any," Nico pointed out.

Sophia made an impatient noise and made a grabby hand gesture at Savio. "You. Pretty boy. Give me some money. That woman there has the best intel on Corfu, but she charges for it."

Nico nodded at Savio. "Give it to her. I'll pay you back."

"I can see a lot has changed in two days," his first lieutenant commented. He handed over a small bag to Sophia.

"Stay here, you two. I don't want her to get scared off by

your sexy glowering." Sophia headed towards the woman, and they quickly hugged and exchanged cheek kisses.

"You want to tell me what is going on, commander?" Savio asked, looking concerned.

Nico gave him the short version of the last few days while he kept watch over Sophia. Not that she could escape with the chain on, but he liked to know where she was. The woman she was chatting to shot him a few curious looks, but money was changing hands.

People liked Sophia; that much was obvious. He was guilty of that too. It had barely taken a day to get her from enemy to ally. And he had kissed her. And he wanted to do it again.

"We found what the Varangians had left of her ship and feared you had gone down with it," Savio said. "We picked up a few survivors and have them on deck, drying out. Sounds like they thought they were dealing with them, and when the quartermaster asked for too much, they decided to blast the hell out of them. The Varangians would rather you be dead than pay for you."

"Good to know. Arkon wants whatever information we can get. Something doesn't feel right about any of this. Varangians using shifter bones for folk magic. What next?"

"I suppose we will find out. Your girl is heading back with a smile on her face."

"She's not my girl," Nico huffed.

"Sure, commander. I'm definitely not smelling her all over you. My mistake."

Nico's serpent liked the idea of having her scent all over it. He really needed that swim to clear his head. There were a few times in his life when his serpent had taken over his body through sheer will. None of them had been pretty.

"Do I have news for you?" Sophia crowed and rejoined them. She tossed the empty bag to Savio.

"Out with it, sea rat. I want to know that it was worth Savio's coin," Nico replied. "Who was the woman?"

"That was Bettina, the owner of the local brothel. Darling woman. Makes a mean cocktail. Anyway, three nights ago she was entertaining some enterprising fellows who had been selling bags of wheat to the Varangians. Turns out they have built themselves quite the camp in the Neretva Delta." Sophia's smile went smug. "And get this—they were also talking about the strange ships that were being built there."

"They must have taken the inventor there," Nico said, rubbing his chin.

"The inventor she kidnapped and sold to them you mean?" Savio asked, tone turning pissy.

"I'm assuming so. Don't pout because I got decent information and you couldn't, Savio," Sophia said.

"That's first lieutenant to you, pirate," he said, eyes narrowing.

Nico ignored their bickering. "We will have to see if there is any truth in this information."

"You can't sail this beast of a battleship in there. They would spot you miles off," Sophia pointed out.

"I'll message Arkon. The last instructions we had were to get you back to Venice. If the Varangians are really building ships, they won't be moving anywhere in a hurry."

"You really need his permission?" Sophia asked, her nose screwing up.

Nico laughed. "Trust me, it's better to keep him in the loop. He's a right prick if he doesn't get his way."

Savio was looking at him like he'd grown another head but said nothing.

"After you, sea rat," Nico said, pointing to the gang plank.

"Fine, but don't you be looking at my ass," she replied, heading up first.

"You're not the captain of this ship," Nico reminded her, most definitely looking at her ass.

"Should I be worried about whatever is going on here?" Savio asked.

"No. It's just...how she is."

"Ah huh."

Nico was about to object when shouts came from the deck, and the chain gave a hard yank. Nico raced up the deck to find a pirate pushing Sophia around.

"You fucking sold us out!" the pirate shouted at her. "Getting revenge for your brother had us running about the Adriatic for months, and the first chance you get, you spread your fucking legs to get yourself out of trouble. You watch your back, bitch, because tonight in the brig, that cunt of yours is—"

Nico exploded, his serpent tearing through any self-control he had remaining. He tackled the pirate to the deck and laid into him. Bone shattered and blood sprayed, but Nico couldn't stop, his rage so drowning and complete. Strong arms came around him and hauled him off what was left of the pirate. He didn't have much of a face, and Nico still wanted more. Wanted to feel flesh between his teeth...

"Commander! Nicolo! Stop!" Savio hissed in his ear. "That is enough."

Nico turned his glare to the other pirates. "Anyone speaks to her like that again, that is what will become of you," he shouted. Every one of them had the sense to look away.

"Commander, give me the cuff and get in the water," Savio urged. "You're about to shift on deck and...and you are scaring her."

Nico turned to Sophia. She was pale and shaking, eyes wide and blood dripping from the corner of her mouth. It was like ice water had been thrown over him.

"Put her in my room and see that she's okay," Nico said. He

pressed the glyphs in the order which released his cuff and passed it to Savio.

"*Nico*," Sophia whispered.

He didn't stop. He kicked off his boots and dived off the side of the ship. The serpent ripped free of him and made for the open sea as fast as it could go.

CHAPTER TEN

S ophia couldn't stop shaking. Savio took her into Nico's
cabin and locked the cuff he was holding to the table
leg. The table was fixed to prevent it from sliding about
in high seas. Not that she thought that she could escape at that
moment, nor did she want to.

"I don't know what you've done to him, but I suggest you
stay where you are and behave for the time being," Savio said.

Sophia nodded. "I swear I haven't done anything to him."

"Except run him in circles for months on end. I don't know
why he hasn't hung you after the grief you've caused him." Savio
handed her a clean handkerchief. "You're bleeding. I'll send in
the med-mage."

"It's only a split lip. I'll be fine," Sophia said, holding the cloth
to her mouth. Roberto had caught her off guard with that
backhand.

"You really think I'm going to defy Nico's orders when he's
in that kind of a mood?" Savio headed for the door. "Don't leave
this cabin. Everyone is too uneasy right now."

Sophia sat down on a couch that looked out at the sea
behind the boat. A slippery, tightening sensation was gripping

her insides. Was Nico okay? She'd never seen such a display of stunning violence. It had taken mere moments for him to cave Roberto's head in. All because he had threatened her.

No one had stood up for Sophia since Tito had died. She should be horrified that Nico had beaten a man to death, but she wasn't. She was gripped by a thousand emotions she didn't understand.

All she had wanted was to kiss his bloody, furious face. That was not the reaction a sane person would have in the same situation, but Sophia knew she hadn't thought of herself as sane when it came to Nico for a long time. She had wondered what he would be like angry, and damn, if it wasn't terrifying and sexy all at once. She wanted to curl around him and purr.

It took the med-mage all of a minute to heal the small cut on her lip and the blossoming bruise. They weren't even game enough to look her in the eye. Nico had freaked out his own crew as well as the pirates.

Well done, prince.

The *Reitia* was out on the open water, sailing north once more, and Sophia worried about Nico being able to find them.

She stared out the windows and spotted ferocious spines cresting the waves behind them. A very big sea serpent was following them. She could now understand why the Varangians were afraid of Nico. He was huge. From what she could see, he was as long as the *Reitia*. Could he stop being so impressive for five bloody seconds? Apparently not.

Was it her serpent blood that made her so drawn to him when clearly it was suicidal? Something had changed since their soft conversation the night before, and him defending her had made that *thing* burst inside of her.

She wished he would come back so she could see that he was okay. She put her head in her hands. Maybe Roberto had been right to accuse her the way he had. It had taken only a handful of days for her to change her mind about Nico.

He had saved her life the night the ship was attacked. He could have let her drown. He could have let Rafail hang her for the pirate she was. At every turn, he had acted in the complete opposite way than she had expected. She couldn't keep hating him after all of that.

The other feeling sliding about inside of her felt just as dangerous. It was lust. Pure, feral lust. She had seen the monster in his eyes, the scales pushing through on his forearms, and had thought, *Yes, there you are. Come out and play with me.*

Sophia went into the cabin's small bathroom and used the full pitcher of water by the basin to wash her face. Her eyes were shining bright and manic. She leaned closer in the mirror. There was gold shining amongst the green that she had never had before.

Was it her serpent side? She tried to think about what the doctor had said all those years ago. Something about how there might be other side effects of her shifter heritage even if she couldn't change into a full serpent form.

Had Nico's meltdown triggered something? He was an alpha after all. Normal humans could feel an alpha's power, but her shifter blood made her experience it on a whole new level. She wanted to lay her head in his lap and submit.

Sophia's teeth ground together. The hell she would. She had never submitted to anyone or anything. She was half human. She could fight that impulse for as long as it was there. It wasn't like as soon as they got to Venice, he wasn't going to hand her over to Arkon and fuck off anyway. Who would protect her once he was gone?

"Shut up," she moaned and clutched her head. "You haven't needed anyone protecting you for years. You were the Pirate King for fuck's sake. Grow the hell up."

Sophia couldn't afford to get any squishy ideas when it came to Nico. Ideas led to emotions, which led to really, really dumb actions. The kind of actions that would get her into trouble. Well, *more* trouble.

She straightened her shoulders and pointed to her reflection.

"You can go back to wherever you've been hiding my entire life, serpent." Her reflection smirked at her, and Sophia quickly looked away. Fuck. This couldn't be happening. She was too old for this kind of nonsense. She would deal with whatever was happening like she always did—by burying it deep down and pretending everything was fine.

* * *

IT WAS LATE, and the moon was high over the inky black water. Sophia had been in Nico's cabin, fighting the urge to go through all of his things. She was actually worrying about him, and that made her furious, so she'd picked up a book and curled up with it.

The door banged open, startling her from her perch on the window seat. Nico's eyes tracked over her, still glowing with his serpent. Someone had given him a towel, but he still gleamed with water. Sophia knew he was built strong, but she wasn't prepared for the dark hair and olive-skinned perfection that was put before her.

Sophia tossed her book at his head. "How dare you just leave like that and make me worry about you!"

Nico caught the book and shut the cabin door. "I thought you were scared of me."

"I wasn't scared. I was a bit surprised when you beat a man to death. Are you a secret psycho or something?" she demanded, closing in on him.

Nico's eyes shone brighter, and the pounding in her core intensified. "It's not a secret. He hurt you. He had to die."

"It was a busted lip. Hardly, life-threatening."

Nico's smile was the most malicious thing Sophia had ever seen. "It was life-threatening for him."

"Oh my god, you are unhinged," she gasped before she closed the distance between them and kissed his furious, glaring face. Nico picked her up and dumped her on the edge of the dining table.

"I'm still not letting you go," he growled against her lips.

"I'm not asking you to," she said, burying her hands in his hair and pulling him back to her mouth.

Nico kissed like a demon, his big hands trailing down her back to her ass before he pulled her up against him. She moaned softly when she felt how hard he was under the towel.

"Better tell me now if you don't want this before it goes any further," he said gruffly, pulling back again. Every part of her was liquid fire. She couldn't stop. Didn't want to. She wrapped her bare legs around his waist.

"I want this," she said. It was all he needed. Nico's mouth devoured hers, his whole body almost shivering with alpha energy. She was drowning in it, and it was the best thing she'd felt in her life. She yanked off his towel and wrapped a hand around his huge dick.

"Wow," she commented.

"Scared?" Nico asked, a teasing edge to his voice. Sophia gave him a hard stroke, making him swear and grip the edge of the table.

"You wish, serpent," she scoffed. Nico ran a hand up her thigh and under the shirt she had been planning to wear to bed.

"You're wearing my shirt," he commented and then immediately distracted her by brushing his fingers over her pussy. His growl echoed deep in his chest.

Sophia didn't care how embarrassingly wet she was. She needed him to get inside of her before she exploded. Nico dragged her to the edge of the table before pushing her down onto it. He lifted her shirt up, exposing her to his heated gaze.

"Fuck," he murmured before he went down on her. Sophia almost slid off the table. Nico grabbed her legs, tugging them over his shoulders.

Gods below, his tongue. She wouldn't have fought with him so much if she'd known what else he could do. His huge hand moved over her stomach, riding the shirt up to free her breasts. He palmed one before tightening his grip.

"Fuck, Nico," she groaned. His other hand went to her clit, thumb pressing in a hard circle as he fucked her with his tongue. Sophia's body rose off the table, her orgasm searing her nerves and making her bite the back of her hand so that the whole damn ship didn't know what was going on.

Sophia didn't get time to recover before Nico was picking her up and pinning her against the wall of the cabin. He grabbed the slack of the chain, bound her wrists together before lifting them over a coat hook.

Sophia was dangling helplessly, but she didn't care. Nico grabbed the collar of her shirt and ripped it in half, tossing the pieces over his shoulder.

"Still with me, sea rat?" Nico asked.

Sophia tried not to smile. "Still waiting on you, you mean."

Nico's husky laugh was pure filth. "I was going to be a gentleman, but you just reminded me who I'm dealing with." Nico grabbed her hips, taking the pressure off her chains. "Bite down on me if you're worried about the crew hearing you scream my name."

"You arrogant—*fuck*," Sophia groaned as Nico slammed his cock into her. She bit into his neck, smothering the cries coming out of her.

"That's it. Bite me harder," he growled. Sophia gasped in a breath before he pounded into her again and again. The newly woken serpent inside of her roared with delight at not just being filled and fucked, but *taken*. He would take every bit of her and leave nothing left for her to hide behind.

Sophia licked up the side of his neck, tasting hot skin and cold sea. She bit into his ear lobe, making him groan.

"Gods, woman, your pussy is magic," he whispered in her ear. "It makes me want to scream too."

Sophia kissed him hard, his eyes brighter than she'd ever seen them. He wasn't fully in control, his beast on the surface, and she loved it.

Following some instinct she couldn't stop to try and understand, she turned her head and offered him her throat. Nico whimpered before thrusting deeper into her. His lips, teeth, and tongue traveled over her neck, making her feel threatened and aroused at the same time. He was a true predator that could end her so easily. One big bite would be all it took.

"Nico," she whispered. She was at her edge, and when she began to topple over it, he bit down hard. Sophia started to sob, her body locking up and releasing, milking him and taking everything he wanted to give her. She smothered her cries into his chest, pleasure and panic all jumbled together.

What had she done? Oh gods, she was going to be ruined. She didn't know if it would be worth it in the long run.

Nico lifted the chain down and carried her over to gently lay her on the bed.

"Don't move," he commanded.

Like she could. She was a mess in every way. He came back with a damp cloth, carefully cleaning her up in gentle strokes. He checked her wrists were okay. A lump built in her throat when he kissed the red marks softly. *Don't be nice to me. You're only going to make it worse.*

Nico lay down beside her and pulled her up against him. She didn't take him for a cuddler. When she tried to move, he growled and dragged her back to him.

"Go to sleep, little pirate, or I'll fuck you again," he grumbled, making her snicker.

Sophia knew it was weakness, but she still curled into him,

letting his heat and big body surround her. His breath tickled her neck as it evened out.

Sophia began to doze in his arms, feeling safe and content for the first time in her tumultuous life. *My mate*, a voice whispered through her.

It was like ice water had been dumped over her. Shaking, Sophia slipped out from under his arm and from the bed. Nico was sprawled out, a happy peaceful look on his sleeping face. She picked up the saber that hung from its place on the wall. It was instinct to find a weapon when she felt threatened.

Mate, the voice inside whispered again. She knew enough about shifters to remember how they felt about mates. She knew what it meant. How their creatures decided for them who their partners would be. It was a life sentence.

This can't be happening. She hurried into the bathroom. Her eyes were fully gold, and she stumbled back away from the sink.

Her clothes were still hanging on the back of the door, so she pulled them on as fast as she could. She stared at the cuff on her wrist. She pressed the series of glyphs she'd watched Nico do earlier that day and held her breath. The cuff opened, and she took it off her wrist and clipped it to the foot of the tub.

Sophia needed to get away and in a hurry. She slung the saber's belt across her chest and tried the window. It swung out silently, and fear compelled her to climb out. The water roared beneath her as she scaled the side of the decorative engravings and headed for the dinghy that was tied to the back of the ship.

Overhead, thunder boomed ominously. Sophia prayed the sounds of the storm would disguise any noise she made. She hurried as the rain began to fall, trying to reach the small boat before everything became too slick to climb.

Go back, the voice inside her insisted. *Mate. Go back!*

"No. *You* go back to sleep and don't bother me again. He won't want us like that. We aren't meant for him," she hissed to herself. She untied the ropes that held the dinghy in place and winched it down into the water. She waited to hear if any alarms had been raised. Nothing. The storm was covering her well. She climbed down the rest of the way and slipped into the dinghy.

"Sorry, Nico. This girl knows when to cut and run," she whispered before she undid the final rope holding her to the ship and let the stern's wake push her out to sea.

CHAPTER ELEVEN

Nico woke suddenly and painfully, his serpent panicking. He sat up and realized he was alone.

"Sophia?" he called. No reply. Nico felt the bed. Cold. He followed the chain from the table to the bathroom. He tapped on the door.

"Sophia? Are you okay in there?" Nico didn't want to bust in on her, but his serpent was thrashing inside of him like it was losing its mind.

"I'm coming in." Nico opened the door and saw the bathroom was empty and the chain cuffed to the tub. "Fuck." He followed her scent to the still open window. The dinghy was gone. "Fuck!"

Nico had enough sense to grab his towel before hurrying out on deck.

"Where is she?" he shouted.

Savio hurried over to him. "What's happened?"

"Sophia is gone. Who the fuck was meant to be on watch?"

"No one has come out of your cabin since you went in after your swim," Savio replied.

Nico ran his hands through his hair. His serpent was tearing apart his insides.

"Commander, please. You're not acting..." Savio began.

Nico dropped his hands, his serpent pushing through enough to growl out, "*Mate*." Nico shoved it back down, but Savio had heard it.

Realization and shock rushed over Savio's face before he turned from Nico.

"Stop the ship! The commander needs to hunt," Savio shouted, and the crew jumped to it.

"Thank you," Nico said.

"Don't go unarmed. She's not right in the head either," Savio replied. Nico had to agree on that.

Did she feel this thing between them was something more than the usual attraction? She had serpent blood after all. Nico went back into his cabin and tossed on a shirt and some pants. He went to reach for his saber and found it gone.

"Goddamn it, Sophia!" he cursed before grabbing his spare and putting it on.

What had he done wrong the night before? He had given her more than one chance to stop, and she hadn't taken it. She had been enjoying it in the moment; he was sure of it. So why had she run? They had made a deal, so she wasn't scared of being hung. It had to be something that he had done.

Find her and then pin her down until she answers you, he decided. His serpent thought it was a good idea.

How much longer was he going to chase this woman? How much longer would his crew take it and not think he was completely incompetent? If it had been any other criminal Nico would have hung them by now. He wouldn't be running about like a lovesick puppy. *Fuck*.

Nico walked back out on deck, and every crew member made sure they were busy.

"We have a tracking sigil on the dinghy to make sure if

it's ever stolen, we can find the culprit," Savio reminded him as they walked to the edge of the ship. "She hasn't disabled it, and she seems to have stopped ten kilometers southeast of us. We will follow you. Whatever you need to sort out between yourselves, I suggest you do it before we get there."

"Thank you, Savio." Nico hesitated, looking at the water below. "I'm sorry to be putting you through all of this."

Savio was trying not to smile. "Goddess willing, it will happen to us all one day. I just hope mine isn't with a troublesome pirate."

"Please don't tell anyone," Nico said, almost begging.

"Not a word, commander. Happy hunting."

Nico was going to give him a raise as soon as they got back to Venice.

Nico dived into the cold water and let the shift come on him. Unlike the brutal way he'd shifted the day before, this was a natural shift that would ensure his clothes and saber survived when he shifted back.

Mate, the serpent hissed and took off through the water, searching. He let it take over. Nico needed not to think, just enjoy the quiet of being under the water. The serpent would find Sophia quicker without his interference.

Ten kilometers wasn't far. She must have stopped running or something had happened to her. The latter thought had his serpent panicking again. Nico couldn't believe that of all the women in the Republic for his serpent to claim, he had to pick her.

Alpha. Mate. Well, no shit she was an alpha. It didn't matter if she could shift or not. She had the charisma, the authority, and arrogance of an alpha. She was beautiful and formidable and a raging pain in his ass. He wanted her back. He wanted her to stop fucking running away from him.

Nico breached the surface of the water and glanced about

him. The dinghy was beached on a tiny sand bank, not even an island.

Sophia saw him, leaped to her feet, and ran to the other side of it. She hadn't bothered to put on shoes. What had she been thinking when she had climbed out of the window? Nico shifted back into his human form and started walking out of the water.

"Nowhere to run, sea rat!" he called. She whirled on him, saber drawn.

"You need to stop coming after me, or I will make you," she snapped, her feet sliding into position.

"I will hunt you to the ends of the earth." Nico raised his sword. "You want to do it the hard way? Fine by me."

Sophia attacked him, quick as a striking snake and just as deadly. Nico met her blow for blow, trying to use his height to his advantage. It didn't matter a whit. Sophia had clearly been fighting people bigger than her for her entire life.

"Tell me why you ran?" he said through gritted teeth. "What changed after I went to sleep, Sophia?"

She made a quick lunge for his side that he had to retreat to avoid. "Maybe I decided that it was better for me to cut my losses?"

"Bullshit. You were with me every step of the way. Something made you freak out and leave me," Nico tried to disarm her, but she anticipated all his tricks. Clearly, Tito had been training her before he died. There was no way she would know all the navy fighting forms otherwise.

Sophia kicked out, aiming for his knee. Nico turned to absorb the impact with his thigh. "Maybe I ran because you were a bad lay."

Nico wasn't going to be goaded. "Maybe you ran because I made you feel something that frightened you."

"Your cock isn't big enough to frighten me," she hissed back. Her eyes flashed golden, and he stumbled back in surprise. She used his temporary lack of balance to disarm him, his saber flying across the other side of the sand bank. He could tackle her and take her down that way. His serpent didn't want to hurt her, and neither did he.

Nico did what an alpha serpent should never do and went to his knees in front of her.

"Kill me if you need to, Sophia."

She had the blade under his chin in a blink. "You don't think I can do it?" she growled. Tears were in those beautiful golden eyes. Gods of the deep, look at her. She was so...perfect.

"I know you can do it, Sophia. You really want to be free of me? This is the only way. Wherever you go, wherever you run, I will hunt you and find you again and again." Nico leaned forward so the tip of the saber dug into his chest. Bright crimson bloomed on the fabric of his shirt.

"Fuck!" Sophia shouted. She plunged the saber in the sand before sitting down beside it. "I hate you so fucking much."

"Stop lying to yourself and to me," Nico replied. He rocked back to sit on the beach beside her. "I know you've got it in you to be coldhearted. You wouldn't have survived this long otherwise. But you're not cold enough to just fuck and run."

"You don't know that," she sniffed, bringing her knees up to her chest. "Stop pretending like you're heartbroken."

"I am a little," Nico replied honestly. "The sex aside, I thought you were starting to trust me."

"It's not you," Sophia admitted, burying her head in her hands.

Nico reached out to touch her, but quickly drew his hand back. He didn't want her picking up the saber again.

"Did something happen with your serpent?" he asked softly. His tongue burned to tell her that she was his mate. The glorious bite bruise on her throat was proof enough that he'd marked her.

"H-How did you know that?" Sophia looked up at him, golden eyes shining.

"Your eyes have changed. I thought you didn't have abilities?"

"I didn't! This thing has just woken up inside of me, and I don't know what's happening to me, Nico! I can't shift, and now I have this...this other part of me that's suddenly there, and I can't control her," Sophia said, launching back to her feet.

Mate, his serpent purred.

Shut up, you're not helping.

Claim mate.

Nico cleared his throat. "Perhaps it's because you are around so many serpents with myself and my crew. It has forced that side of you to finally present itself."

"I can't shift. I don't have the magic, so why the hell do I have this stupid voice inside of my head?" she demanded, turning to him. She was freaking out, both sides of her warring with herself.

"Let me help, Sophia," he said, getting back to his feet. "It's common with shifters when their beasts start to make themselves known. I can settle it if you let me."

Very slowly so she wouldn't lash out, Nico pushed out his alpha power. His abilities were one of the reasons he could have so many shifters under his command and avoid bloodshed.

He didn't want to dominate her, just calm her. He held out his hand to her. Sophia's shoulders slumped, and with a growl of pure frustration, she took his hand.

"There we are. It's going to be okay," Nico said, sinking his alpha power into his voice. He drew her closer, and she crashed into him with a sob.

"You tell anyone I cried, I'll fucking flay you," she said against his chest.

Nico put his arms around her. "Not a word. No more running, Sophia. Please. There's too much at stake."

"Why do you even care? You're just going to dump me in the

doge's prison for Arkon to interrogate and leave anyway," she said.

Nico pressed his nose into her hair and inhaled her scent. His own serpent finally calmed down, and he could smell the change in her. She smelled like a shifter. Their scents were all mingled together, and his arms tightened around her.

"I'm not going to leave you in any prison. Even if I did, you would talk Arkon into letting you go in less than an hour. I'm not going to abandon you," he tried to reassure her. "You need to trust me, just a little. Please stop running from me."

Sophia softened into him, a sweet sigh of surrender coming out of her. "Don't betray me, Nico."

"I won't." Nico pulled back from her and wiped the tears off her cheeks. "Don't cry, little pirate. My ship is coming, and I don't want you losing your fearsome reputation."

Sophia let him go. "*Stop* being so nice to me. It's not helping."

"Don't tell me what to do. You're not my captain," Nico replied, smiling despite himself. This woman would drive him to the brink with her antics, and he still couldn't wait to see what she did next.

The sun was setting when the *Reitia* appeared. Savio had taken his sweet time, but Nico knew it was for him.

"If you want me to trust you, no more cuffs," Sophia said as they got into the dinghy.

Nico nodded. "They didn't hold you anyway."

Sophia smiled at him. It was big and beautiful. "No, they did not."

"Swear to me you won't run," Nico said, stopping his rowing. Her smile slipped as she thought about it. Nico didn't move. He needed something—anything—to believe that she would do as she promised.

"I swear on the memory of my brother that I won't run again unless I believe my life is seriously in danger," she said solemnly. Nico knew that was about as good as it would get.

AMY KUIVALAINEN

"Fair enough. Don't expect the crew to be happy about being delayed again on your behalf," Nico warned her. He picked up the oars and began to row.

Sophia stared openly at his arms flexing, and he tried to think about anything except for her spread out on his dining table.

"Your crew aren't stupid enough to mutiny against you. Not after you fucked up Roberto yesterday," she pointed out. She didn't look like she gave two shits what other people thought about her. Alpha through and through.

"Just behave until we get to Venice, and I will give you a crown to match all the gold Gio will give you," Nico replied.

Sophia's serpent eyes sparkled at him. "*Now*, you have got yourself a deal, D'Argento."

CHAPTER TWELVE

Nico's crew were clearly better trained than Sophia's ever were because not one person gave her a second look once they climbed aboard. Savio followed them into Nico's cabin and shut the door.

"Have you two decided on an agreement, or shall I lock Lady Osara in her cell below deck?" he asked Nico.

"Lady Osara? My, don't I feel fancy," Sophia said, sitting down at the dining table where someone had placed food and wine. Everyone seemed to want to feed Nico, and she was happy to take advantage of that.

"You should be feeling grateful that the commander wishes for your safety," Savio said coolly. "I would have left you on the island."

Sophia hummed and ate some grapes but ignored his bitchy tone. Maybe Nico should put her below deck. She had already fucked up once. He didn't seem dumb enough to give her too much freedom again.

Nico placed both of his sabers back on their racks. "She will be staying in here, but we will need some extra blankets and pillows. And Savio? Some more food. I didn't eat when I was in the water," he said, and Savio went out without another word.

Sophia waited until he was gone before looking over at Nico. "We are done playing one bed?"

"You'll fit on the couch by the windows just fine." Nico poured himself some wine. His smile turned roguish, and her lady bits clenched. "You want back in my bed, sea rat? You're going to have to earn it."

Sophia couldn't argue with that. She could tell that she had hurt him by leaving. It was a dick move, and she knew it. She had gotten as far as the tiny island before she'd had a panic attack about being so far from him. She had reacted without thinking. She hadn't packed supplies. Or shoes. There was a high possibility that she would have died if Nico hadn't come looking for her.

When his huge head surfaced, she had felt two things—the urge to piss her pants at how terrifying he was in his sea serpent form and indescribable relief. He had come for her. She had fucked him and run away, and *still*, he had come for her. Her newly awoken serpent was thrilled with the idea that he would chase her down again and again.

"You can be angry if you need to be, Nico. I don't blame you. Just don't change your tune if I decide to sleep naked," she said, stealing more grapes from his plate.

"Back at you. I do sleep naked. Let's not forget, you were the one who launched herself at me last night," Nico pointed out.

For the first time since Sophia was a teenager, she blushed. "It was all part of the plan."

"Sure it was, pirate. Your plan seemed really well thought out. No food, no water, no hat or shoes."

They were interrupted by a crew member bringing in another platter of food, plus pillows and a blanket. Sophia smiled and thanked the man, but he just nodded to Nico and didn't say a word.

"Wow. They are pissed," she said, filling up a plate. She had been starving on that stupid little island.

"Cautious of me more than you. Your scent has changed and that makes them...wary," Nico explained.

Sophia lifted the front of her shirt and sniffed. "Yeah, I could use a bath."

"It's not just that. You smell like a serpent today when yesterday you didn't. Have you really never felt that side of yourself?" Nico asked. There was a delicious hum of alpha radiating around him, and it made Sophia want to curl up in his lap and soak in it like a hot bath.

Sophia reached for wine, but Nico pushed water at her instead. "Drink that first. You were in the sun all day."

"Fine. And to answer your question, no, I haven't felt the pushy bitch inside of me until the last two days. My eyes are doing this weird thing too where they are changing color," she said and drank her water. "It's what freaked me out so much."

Nico gestured to her to lean forward. "Let me have a proper look."

Sophia swallowed the bread she was chewing and drew nearer to him. His large hand lifted her chin, touch as gentle as it had ever been. She really had been an idiot to run from him.

I tried to stop you, her serpent grumbled.

"What happened there? They were green, and then they changed to gold," Nico said.

"She decided to get opinionated."

"About?"

Kiss him, the voice urged. *Mate, mate, mate.*

"It likes it when you are near because you're an alpha," she lied.

Nico's eyebrow rose. He would be able to smell a lie. Literally. And she did it anyway. "No other reason?"

Sophia shook her head. "N-Nope."

Nico brushed a thumb over her cheek and let her go. "You are sunburnt. I have some balm that will help."

"I'm fine. Stop fussing, or people will think that you care," she said, reaching for the wine before grabbing the water instead.

She didn't trust whatever was happening to her. If she added alcohol to that mix... It seemed like a good way to fuck up.

"The changes that are happening usually happen during puberty, but I think you are fine. I suppose it's triggered because I'm an alpha. When we get to Venice, we can check if you like. For now, know that the serpent is perfectly natural, and you will be fine," Nico said before going back to his dinner. He must've been hungry because between them, they finished off a prodigious amount of food.

"If you want a hot bath, I can have it arranged," Nico said. "But you'll have to keep the door open. I don't want you going out the window again."

"I don't want to piss off the crew any more than I already did. I'll have it cold. I'm going to steal one of your shirts, seeing how you destroyed the last one," Sophia said with a grin. It was now a fond memory.

"It was worth the sacrifice at the time. You know where to find them," Nico said, dismissing her.

At the time. Sophia tried not to flinch.

Nico moved to a desk on the other side of the room and started writing in a logbook and reading missives.

Sophia didn't like being ignored, but he was a commander, and that did have its duties. Ones that she had distracted him from the last few days.

She tried to summon her old devil-may-care attitude, but it didn't make an appearance. She knew she wouldn't get any more chances, and that made her want to tread carefully for the first time in her life.

I'm only doing it for the gold, she told herself. She bathed and changed before making up a bed on the window couch. The book that she had been reading the night before was still there, so she picked it up again.

It felt weirdly domestic and...nice. She had been a captain, but unless it was a meeting with Kyrios, she was alone in her cabin. She felt curiously comfortable in Nico's presence. The only sounds were the waves outside and the slight scratching of Nico's pen against the paper.

It was late when Nico finally stopped and went into the bathroom. Sophia was rather disappointed that he didn't bathe with the door open. She almost swallowed her tongue when he walked out buck naked. Gods, he was brutally and beautifully made.

"What are you staring at, sea rat?" he asked, making her jump.

"My book," she replied, looking so hard at the page, she was surprised it didn't catch on fire. Well, two could play at that game.

"Bedtime, is it? Good idea. It's been a long day." She pulled off the shirt she was wearing and dropped it on the decking. She could feel Nico's gaze traveling over her like a hot touch.

"Get the lamps, would you, commander?" she said before rolling over to face the windows, giving him a view of her bare back and ass.

After a long moment, the cabin went dark, and Nico got into bed. She tried not to giggle when she heard him swear softly. It was good to know she wasn't going to suffer alone.

CHAPTER THIRTEEN

Nico was going to murder whoever was arguing outside of his door. He dragged himself out of sleep enough that he recognized the voices.

"You can't go in there. It's a violation of privacy, *habibi*."

"It's a violation of my patience that they have been fucking about the Adriatic for days instead of coming home like they were ordered to."

Nico sat up, suddenly wide-awake and alarmed. Surely his ears were deceiving him.

"Nico?" Sophia whispered sleepily. "What's wrong?"

"Put your shirt on, sea rat. We are about to have company."

Nico dragged on his pants and was halfway to the door when it sprang open. A wild haired sorcerer and an unapologetic djinn king came on in. Zahir was looking particularly magnificent in a peacock blue robe, his gold jewelry glinting in the morning sun.

"You see, Zahir, I told you they were awake," Arkon declared. Both of the men's sharp eyes fixed on Sophia. She didn't seem intimidated in the least standing in only Nico's shirt. "Okay, *now*

I get why you were dragging your feet. You didn't tell me she was a redhead. I love redheads!"

Zahir looked her over. "So you are the woman who has caused me and my consort so much grief in the last few weeks."

Nico moved in front of Sophia, but she pushed around him.

"I am really sorry about that," she said to Zahir. "I didn't know he was a mage. He told me he wanted to meet with some 'old friends.' I would have never taken him to Venice if I had known his plans were to fuck with the djinn. Even I'm not that suicidal."

Nico snorted. "But you would antagonize me, sea rat?"

"He is a real threat," Sophia said, gesturing at Zahir. " You are just...you."

Zahir's animosity was wavering. God, she was charming him too. "What did the mage promise you to get him into the city?"

"The usual deal I couldn't refuse—a ship, a bag of gold, and the plans of the D'Argento mansion in Castello. I needed to prove to my crew I could get in and out of the city."

Nico put his hands on his hips. "So you could come back and rob me? Woman, you are unbelievable."

"The *silver* serpent implies silver, prince," Sophia replied. "I didn't see why not."

"Damn it, I like her. I can't stay mad at her especially when she makes you smile like that, Nicolo," Zahir said with a soft laugh. "What did you spend the money on?"

"I gave it to the San Gerolamo Orphanage because the posh boys in Castello never give them donations even though they love making orphans with this dumb war," Sophia replied.

Arkon grinned. "Wanting to steal from Nico to give to orphans. Aw, now I like her too."

"You would," Nico snapped.

Arkon ignored him, his charming smile on Sophia. "Have you ever thought about being a spy, my dear?"

"I don't think you can afford me," Sophia replied.

"Oh, I bet I could." Arkon turned his attention back to Nico. "Dom and Stella are hustling your cook for some breakfast. Put a shirt on before you start to make me feel insecure about my masculinity."

"Allow me to help you feel more comfortable, my dear," Zahir said to Sophia and snapped his fingers. Instantly, she was dressed in a dark blue and silver kimono.

D'Argento colors, Nico realized, his heart going erratic. He shook himself and got his shirt on just as Dom and Stella arrived with breakfast.

"I told you they wouldn't wait," Stella said before turning to Sophia. "I'm so sorry for their rudeness."

Sophia laughed. "This is not my idea of rude."

"What are you all doing here? Apart from waking me up?" Nico asked, sitting down at the head of the table. They could have warned him they were coming at least.

"Arkon thought you were taking too long to get to Venice, and Savio sent a message saying you were going to be delayed even more," Dom replied, sitting beside Nico and pouring himself coffee. "The sorcerer threw a tantrum and demanded Zahir teleport us to you instead."

"I did not throw a tantrum! This pirate has intel on the Wolf Mage and the Varangians. It's important to the war effort," Arkon argued. He was definitely pouting.

Nico ran a hand over his face. It was too early for this. "At least let me have coffee first."

He poured Sophia a cup and handed it to her before helping himself. Dom's head tilted to one side as he watched them, his golden eyes curious.

"I hear you've given our Nico quite the chase, Sophia. I'd love to hear more about that," Stella said, sharing a look with Dom.

Damn it. They knew. How did they know? Nico gave them

both warning looks to keep their mouths shut. They both had the audacity to smirk at him.

"Me first," Arkon interrupted, he patted the chair next to him. "Come and sit with me, gorgeous Sophia, and tell me all your delicious secrets. You can whisper them in my ear."

Nico let out a warning growl before he could check himself. Everyone froze, except for Arkon whose smile widened at the threat. He played the fool, but he was a stone-cold bastard when he wanted to be.

Arkon tutted. "Don't act like a beast, Nicolo. No wonder she keeps running away from you."

"The Great Hunt," Zahir whispered, dark eyes widening in surprise. "Oh, I see. How delicious."

Sophia looked at him. "Am I missing something?"

"Nothing important. You men are boring, so we are leaving," Stella declared suddenly, hooking her arm around Sophia's and leading her towards the door. "Let's drink our coffees on deck and let the men talk Council business."

"Good idea," Sophia said. She paused to re-fill her cup and gestured at Zahir. "Hey, magic fingers, mind giving me some real clothes?"

Magic fingers, Arkon mouthed at Nico, eyes full of mischief. Nico was going to toss the sorcerer into the ocean by the end of the day; he just knew it.

Zahir laughed, deep and rich. His magic danced about Sophia, and she was dressed in boots, navy pants, and a long sleeve shirt in seconds. When she turned her back, there was a serpent stitched on the back in blue and silver. A serpent that looked a lot like Nico. Seeing her dressed in his colors again was doing strange things to his insides.

"I like you. I'm sorry again about the Varangian," Sophia said, shooting Zahir a saucy wink before heading out into the sun with Stella.

As soon as they were alone, Nico put his head in his hands. "I hate you all so much. My house colors, Zahir? Really?"

The djinn king shrugged. "All of your men know who she belongs to anyway. Why not make it official? I really like her. Very annoying, considering the revenge plans I had. I suppose you must like her too because she's still breathing, and she's half naked in your cabin."

"I can smell your scent all over her, so your serpents will too," Dom added, his smile widening. "You had better start talking before they come back."

Nico opened his mouth and said the one thing he shouldn't have been telling anyone. "She's my mate and my serpent is freaking out and I don't know what to do." He was panicking just saying it out loud.

The three men at the table had become his closest friends, and if he couldn't tell them what was really happening, he couldn't tell anyone.

To keep Arkon from fretting, Nico told them about the information Madam Bettina on Corfu had given Sophia, as well as Sophia's escape the day before.

"I've never heard of such a late awakening for a shifter, but perhaps it's the mating bond that's causing it," Dom said after Nico was finished. "The chase is definitely a part of the courting ritual."

"Nico's mating can wait. Can you go after the inventor? The boat building happening at the coast is a new problem we haven't planned for," Zahir said, toying with his earring. "Especially if they are going to be using them to hunt serpents. Using shifter bodies for magic is disturbing. It's what is troubling me most. So many magic users have come into the Republic, fleeing the persecution, but many have not. I shudder to think that they have been hunted in order to be harvested."

"And we had so many unregistered users traded to the

Varangians by my fucking father," Dom added, looking pissed. "None of this is making sense."

"We deal with the ship building first and go from there." Nico got up to pace. He didn't like Sophia out of his sight, and gods only knew what mischief Stella and she would get into. "We can do a quick recon of the camps, but Sophia said that the ship would be spotted too quickly."

"Take her with you," Arkon suggested. Nico glared at him. "What? It's her fault that the inventor was taken at all. She broke it, so she can fix it."

"You want me to take my mate into a Varangian war camp? Are you insane?" Nico growled, his nostrils flaring.

"You aren't mated yet. You haven't even told her. She's not yours," Arkon pointed out.

Nico snarled at him. *The hell she wasn't. She was his mate.*

"Enough," Dom interrupted. "I understand your reluctance, Nico, but Sophia is not exactly made of glass. She probably knows how to get in and out of their settlement without being seen better than you would. Arkon is being a dick about it, but he's not wrong. She needs to help fix this mess if she's ever going to be welcome back in Venice."

Dom gave Nico a meaningful look, and Nico felt like he'd been kicked. If Sophia was ever going to be his mate officially, they had to prove to Gio that they could trust her. As a D'Argento, she would be politically tied to the city that she had betrayed. Nico felt like an idiot for even considering the mating, especially because they could barely be in the same room without fighting. The real problem was that his serpent had decided for him, and now he would never be able to let her go.

"Perhaps we should be drinking something stronger than coffee," Zahir said, reading Nico's distress far too easily.

"No. We need clear heads to make some proper plans," Arkon replied, and they all stared at him in surprise. "What? I can behave myself when it's important. Go and fetch your pretty lady pirate, Nico, so I can pump her for information."

"Mention her and pumping again in the same sentence, and I'll break your nose, sorcerer."

"Oh, I do love it when you get saucy, Nico." Arkon laughed, but it didn't reach his eyes. "Now, do as I fucking tell you."

CHAPTER FOURTEEN

Sophia followed Stella up the staircase to the ship's wheel. Savio nodded politely to Stella but still looked suspiciously at Sophia. She supposed she deserved it.

They stood at the back of the ship to look at the waves and the sun. It was a beautiful morning, and Sophia was happy to be out on the water.

"So, which are you? Carrot or the stick?" she asked Stella.

Sophia had heard about the Aladoro mate. She was pretty, feisty, and had an explosive kind of lightning magic that hadn't been seen in centuries.

"I'm neither. I didn't want to listen to the men bitch at each other. They need a good twenty minutes riling each other before any work can get done," Stella said with a fond smile. "You've really given Nico the runaround, and they will need to tease him about it."

Sophia took a sip of her coffee. "I can't say it wasn't fun while it lasted. Why would they tease him about it?"

"Nico is... How to put this... He can be quite a serious sort of person. The fact you've been driving him into rages only to now be teasing and laughing with you? It's like a different side of him. A rare side that he doesn't show very often." Stella leaned back against the ship's railing. "Maybe because you are both serpents?"

"I'm not a serpent. I'm half, and I can't shift," Sophia replied.

"You think that matters?"

"Not to me, but it does to people like them," Sophia said, pointing to the crew, who were throwing curious glances their way.

Stella smiled. "I get it. I'm human, but I'm the mate of one of the most powerful shifters in the Republic. I didn't think it would work either."

"But it does?" Sophia had to ask. Her serpent was erratic, and it wanted Nico every second she had her eyes open. It was going to be hard to ignore the tentative bond growing between them. No matter how angry he was at her.

"It does. There are some things more important to the shifters than status and wealth. Mates are...sacred. Off limits. No questions asked," Stella tried explaining. Her clever eyes were studying Sophia. "Anything else you need to know?"

She wasn't outright asking about Nico, but Sophia could read between the lines. Stella knew. Somehow.

"Did you feel like you were losing your mind?" she asked. She rested her forearms on the wooden railing beside her. "Like you go from hating them but needing them and wanting to make them as angry as possible?"

Stella tipped back her head and laughed. It was a good laugh that made Sophia grin just from hearing it. "Yes, that's normal. It made the sex pretty explosive."

Sophia blew out a long breath that had Stella's brows shooting up.

"No. Really?"

"Shhh, remember they can hear us," Sophia said, nodding toward the crew.

Stella quickly turned to face the water so they couldn't see her face.

"I didn't think it had gone that far," she whispered.

"It did, but I fucked it up. Now, he won't trust me again and is still pissed off," Sophia replied. She wanted to bang her head against the railing.

"He will get over it, trust me. Predator shifters love the chase. It's their favorite game. Maybe hold off running again until they figure out what to do about the Varangians making ships," Stella suggested. "Nico will come around. Just give him time."

The back of Sophia's neck tingled with awareness as the shifter himself walked up the stairs. His long hair was still out and windswept, making him look like a pirate's wet dream. He gave her a long suspicious look.

"Why am I suddenly worried you are trying to recruit Stella into stealing my ship?" he asked.

Sophia pointed to her chest. "Me, commander? I would never dream of doing a thing like steal this beautiful, big warship."

"No? You have a bigger prize in mind?" he asked, a small smirk beginning in the corner of his mouth.

"Only your heart, handsome," Sophia said with a big wink.

Nico grunted. "Good luck with that. Arkon wants to speak with you two. You better be feeling in a truthful mood, sea rat."

"Ever the charmer, Nicolo," Stella said with a shake of her head. She headed down the stairs, leaving them alone.

"Don't suppose you want to tell me how angry they are before I go in?" Sophia asked.

Nico's smirk became a smile. "Angry? Zahir was ready to torture you in ways only djinn know how for that shit the Varangian mage put him through. It took a whole five seconds before he changed his mind. Arkon has already become close to be murdered like five times for his suggestive comments about you."

Sophia dared to take a step closer to him so she could smell his aftershave and sea scent. The twisting thing inside of her settled as soon as it hit her lungs.

"Why would you care what Arkon says? You've made it clear how you feel about me," Sophia replied.

Nico's eyes glowed sapphire. "Yes, I have, which means if you think I'm going to let anyone else have you, then you misunderstand the situation."

"Maybe I do." Sophia's heart fluttered in a way that it really shouldn't have. It was too dangerous and impossible. She quickly made for the stairs.

"Sophia?"

She turned and looked up at him. "Yes?"

"Were you really going to try to rob my house in Castello?" he asked.

"Be nice or I still might," she replied. God, she loved the way he looked so confused and angry at the same time. She really wasn't right in the head to keep goading him. She never knew when to stop, so she added, "Apparently, you have great family jewels."

"You would know." Nico's nostrils flared as he breathed in her scent. His smile made her pussy clench. "And we both know how much you liked them."

"I could've liked them a lot more, but alas, you hate me again. We had best go and see what the Grand Sorcerer wants," she said and hurried down the stairs. Flirting with Nico was always going to backfire on her because he knew exactly what he did to her body. Stupid shifter noses.

In the cabin, Arkon was arguing with Zahir, and Stella was sitting casually in Dom's lap. They looked like they were friends hanging out and not members of the Republic's most feared Council of Ten.

"Here they are. If you two are done sparring with each other, we could get on with it," Arkon said. "Tell me what you know about the Varangians you've been dealing with, Sophia."

She sat down and grabbed some of the fruit and bread left on Nico's plate. Sophia knew that she could play about with Nico, but she wasn't dumb enough to be difficult to the Grand Sorcerer. She would give them the whole truth and nothing less.

"They deal with pirates and smugglers a lot. Especially when it comes to food supplies," she replied. "The inventor was a bounty job that they offered to anyone who could pull it off."

"Where did you deliver them?" Dom asked.

Sophia turned to Nico, who had taken up position behind her chair. "Do you have maps of the Dalmatian coast I can use?"

Nico fetched them, and they cleared a space on the dining table. Sophia grabbed a salt shaker and placed it on the map. "I dropped the inventor and his daughter off here. It's a small village called Lovište. If Bettina's information is good, and it always is, then the Varangians have started building their boats here at Rogotin at the mouth of the river. There's a fortress there with a watchtower that the officers use. The soldiers are spread out through what remains of the town."

"I knew they had gotten a foothold on part of the coast, but I didn't know it was the whole city," Arkon grumbled.

"You don't get out of Venice much, do you, sorcerer?" she asked.

"Not if I can help it."

"Then that's your problem. Your spies can't be as good as everyone claims if you didn't know they had taken Rogotin."

"I knew it as a name on a missive. Besides, my spies have been busy trying to track down the unregistered magic users that were sold off to the Varangians. You wouldn't know anything about that, would you?" the sorcerer asked. His tone was polite enough, but Sophia saw straight through it.

"Fuck you. I don't deal with slaves. The inventor was a

bounty, and it wasn't my idea to sell him to the Varangians. My crew outvoted me," Sophia snapped.

"Bounty or not, he was an innocent like his daughter."

"A man who is making war machines and building battleships is not innocent. I didn't know the daughter was with him, and by the time I did, it was too late. My quartermaster had made the deal. I wanted to ransom them to Nico to lure him out of Venice. It all got...fucked up on the way," Sophia replied. She wouldn't let anyone, especially a bunch of rich people, judge her for the choices she had made to survive. She didn't dare look at Nico. He'd thought the worst of her too when it came to the inventor. She couldn't let the fuck-ups in her past get to her because otherwise she would drown in them.

"Getting back on track," Zahir said, clearing his throat. "Are you familiar with Rogotin? Do you think there would be a way in?"

Sophia wrinkled her nose. "With a warship? No. I wouldn't go anywhere near there. One or two people? If they were dressed as locals? Then maybe. The Varangians took over, which pissed people off, but they are farmers and fishermen. They aren't soldiers. They have *recruited* local people to cook and clean up at the fortress, but their guards don't really notice them."

Sophia grabbed a piece of paper and pencil from Nico's desk and started to draw a rough map of the town and where she knew the soldiers had made barracks.

"How do you know all of this?" Nico asked.

"I scoped the place about eighteen months ago when Kyrios first suggested dealing with the empire occasionally. There were no ships being built then, but there was plenty of space to do it. I don't know how many soldiers are there now," Sophia replied. She pointed at the islands all along the coast. "It's definitely a good place to hide for them. Unless you know how to sail through them, these islands can be tricky. Lots of places to hide ships, lots of places for ambushes."

"That settles it. You will take Nico and go and rescue the inventor and see how many ships we are dealing with," Arkon said, knocking on the table.

"I don't like it. Sophia isn't a soldier," Nico began.

"No shit. I'm a smuggler, which means I'm going to be a lot better than you with a job like this," Sophia argued. "I know there's no way I can talk you out of going, Nico, but I'm not letting you go alone. They would make you as a spy in half a minute."

Nico frowned. "I'll dress as a fisherman."

"They would still catch you! You don't hold yourself like one, and you don't talk like one." Sophia rubbed a hand over her face. "You could wear a sack, and everyone would still know you were a rich boy because you don't know how to do humble. I should do this alone."

"Over my dead body," Nico growled. "I don't trust you not to run off the first chance you're out of my sight."

Sophia flinched. The other people at the table all pretended to be interested in something else.

"Anything you can tell me about the Wolf Mage?" Arkon asked, changing the subject.

"Last thing I heard was that she and Emperor Arkadi weren't getting along. It was making the soldiers uneasy because they might fear the emperor, but they love their saint," Sophia replied, ignoring Nico and his sexy glower.

Arkon rolled his eyes. "If that woman is a saint, then I'm the pope."

"Doesn't matter what you believe. The commoners believe in her power. It makes children uneasy when their parents are fighting. If they ever had a true falling-out, I think Arkadi wouldn't have the support he imagines."

Arkon rubbed at the stubble on his chin. "Interesting, but only if it's true."

Sophia shrugged. "It's only what I heard."

"We will see what we can find out on our scouting trip," Nico said, and she shook her head in despair.

Asking questions in a town run by the Varangians? It was nothing but a fast way to die.

CHAPTER FIFTEEN

By nightfall they had a plan. It wasn't the best plan that Sophia had ever had, but it wasn't the worst either.

"The next crew I have, I'm getting a djinn," she said to Zahir. He had teleported them from the ship to a road leading down from the hills and into Rogotin. He'd also helped them with some more clothing that was favored by the Croatian peasants, though Sophia still thought they looked too clean, and she hated wearing a dress.

"Put this on, Nico. I can use it to track you if anything goes wrong," Zahir said. It was a small pendent of the Wolf Mage in her saintly aspect. He gave Sophia a stern look. "Look after him."

"I'll try my best."

Zahir laughed softly. "Don't die." And then, he was simply gone.

"Yeah, definitely getting a djinn. They are handy for getting about fast," she said, staring at the empty road.

"Or you could honor our agreement and not go back to piracy at all," Nico said. He looked good as a peasant. Too good. Maybe Sophia was a little biased. She tried to straighten the tight short vest that went over her plain dress.

"Stop playing with it," Nico said, watching her struggle.

"Easy for you to say. It's not your tits being squished up so you look like a slutty milk maid," Sophia grumbled.

"Turn around," Nico replied, and she did. He undid the laces and retied them for her so they weren't so tight. "Better?"

"Yes. Um, thanks," she said, trying not to think about him undressing her.

"We had best get moving," he said gruffly.

Sophia took the lead, and she tried not to think how crazy it was that she was about to willingly take the Republic's most infamous commander right into a Varangian war camp.

It was a half an hour walk into the town, so Nico decided it was a good time to pry into her business.

"You never told me that you were going to ransom the inventor back to me," he said.

"What does it matter? He still went to the Varangians," she replied, not slowing her pace down. A moonlit walk on a road into enemy territory wasn't a great place to have a heart-to-heart.

"It matters to me. You let me think you were selling out the Republic to them."

"You're going to think that anyway, so I don't see why it matters. It was still my crew that handed him and his daughter over to them. The fact I'm trying to get them back now is utter lunacy, but I wasn't going to let you do this alone," Sophia replied. The lights of the town were coming into view. Hopefully, the path through the old farms wasn't guarded.

"I appreciate that," Nico replied. There was a softness in his voice that made her turn.

"Don't go nice on me, Nico, or I won't respect you as much," she huffed. She could just make out his smile in the moonlight.

"My mistake. As you were, sea rat," he said, and she shook her head at him.

"This way. We need to get off the main road," she said and

94

began to cut across a field. There was a time, she remembered, when little houses dotted the coast, but after the Varangians came, most people who could afford to flee had done so. The ones who were too stubborn to run had to live with being occupied.

"Use those magical eyes of yours to make sure I don't step in a ditch," she whispered.

It took her a few moments to orientate herself, but Sophia found her way through the remnants of the overgrown orchard and climbed over a wooden fence. They slipped unseen into the town, and Nico drew closer to her.

There were Varangian banners hanging from flag poles and from balcony railings. The fort had been built in the first three months. It was an squat building made of gray concrete blocks. It had a tall watchtower, and the whole complex sat like an ugly crab on the waterfront. They made their way down to the docks, blending in with night workers getting ready to get on fishing boats.

"Fuck, look at them," Nico whispered. He pointed across the river where five boats had been built already. Sophia didn't have his eyesight, but she could make out the skeleton like hulls for ten more. "We are going to need to stop this before they get any further along."

"Focus, Nico. Unless we get the inventor, they will be able to make more," she whispered, squeezing his hand.

Nico nodded and unclenched his jaw. She could already see his mind making battle plans.

"Let's see if we can find a friendly face," Sophia suggested and headed for the tavern. She had been there with Kyrios, and the owner recognized her on sight. Blago didn't care who they were if they spent money. It was one of his more redeeming features.

The tavern looked quiet for that time of night, but Sophia tried not to let it bother her too much. It could mean anything. She paused by the door. "Keep your mouth shut. Let me talk."

"Following your lead," Nico replied, and her heart did a double beat. He was actually going to trust her? Wonders never ceased.

Inside was crowded with fishermen and dock workers. They used to spill out onto the streets, but maybe the appearance of so many extra soldiers in town made them wary of becoming too rowdy.

Sophia wended her way through the tables and patrons until she reached the corner of the bar. Blago was a huge man with a big black beard and not a hair on his shaved head. His dark eyes landed on Sophia, and he nodded to a waitress to take his place at the bar.

"Beautiful, captain. It's been too long since I've seen you," Blago said, taking her by the shoulders and kissing both of her cheeks. His eyes went to Nico. "Who is your friend?"

"A new crew member I picked up in Cyprus. He's big and pretty and doesn't talk," Sophia said, smiling at him.

"Sounds like the perfect man for you, my sweet."

"You got time to talk in private?" she asked.

Blago held out a hand towards the door behind the bar. "Always have time for you, Captain Osara," he replied. "Should we leave your pretty friend out here?"

"Oh, no, he's loyal. He can come," Sophia said and followed Blago.

"Your quartermaster still giving you grief?"

"Nope. Kyrios got himself killed in a skirmish," she replied.

Blago sat behind his big desk and gestured to the seat opposite. "What can I do for the Pirate King this fine evening?"

"Rogotin has gotten busy since I was here last. Tense too," she said, getting comfortable. Nico leaned his back against the door like the good bodyguard he was.

"These fucking Varangians aren't good for business. They are cheap and nasty. The extra soldiers that came to build their boats are assholes. Came from Kyiv, a present from the emperor."

"Who's running them these days? What happened to the jolly fat guy?"

"Don't know, but a vicious shit of a man has taken his place. Name is Leonid Siderov. He's an ambitious navy man from the sounds of things. Stationed here to build their ships to take on the Republic."

Sophia pulled out a bag of coin. "This is for you if you can tell me where they have locked up the inventor that Kyrios sold them."

"You want him back? What for?" Blago asked.

Sophia grinned. "I've had a good counteroffer. If he's gone, that means the Varangians will build their boats somewhere else."

Blago pulled on his beard and gestured to her. Sophia tossed him the bag. "They are keeping him at the old customs house, not far from here. There is a small staff of women that clean and cook for him and the soldiers that are stationed there. That will be your way in. Your big friend will have to wait outside. He's too obvious. They change their guards at midnight."

"Blago, you are the best," Sophia said, beaming at him.

"I'm tired of the fuckers in my town. I hope the leaders of the Republic get their shit together and get the Varangians out of Croatia already. Everything is going to shit," Blago complained.

Sophia held out a hand to him, and Blago clasped it. "Don't worry, old friend. I have it on good authority that the Republic has plans already under way. You know they don't like to share their oceans."

Blago grunted. "About damn time. Watch yourself, Sophia. These new soldiers can't be reasoned with like the old ones. They are extremists."

"Thank you," Sophia said. She got to her feet and headed for the door. "It's been good weather lately. Why don't you go north for a few days and tell your staff to do the same."

Blago was a friend, and his tavern was way too close to the harbor. If Nico and the Republic decided to come and bomb Rogotin to hell, Blago was in the firing line.

Blago's bushy brows went up. "I don't know what trouble you're in now, captain, but thank you. I have a sister in Split I haven't seen for six months, and I could use a holiday."

"Good man," Sophia said, and Nico opened the door for her. Once they were outside again, he whispered, "Was that wise to warn him? He could turn around and tell the first soldier he sees."

"He won't. Blago is a survivor, and he fled to Croatia to get away from the empire. He has more of a reason to hate them than you do," Sophia replied.

The old customs house looked more like a holiday villa than a government building. It was made of golden sandstone and had pretty gardens. It also had a high wrought iron fence with a back gate leading into an alley. Two Varangian soldiers dressed in their gray uniforms stood watch. Sophia had nabbed a wicker washing basket from the back of someone's house and now had it resting on her hip. All she had to do now was convince the soldiers to let her in.

"I don't want you going in there alone," Nico said, grabbing her hand.

Sophia took a deep breath. "Nico, I will be fine. I have done far more dangerous things than this over the years. I have two daggers hidden under these skirts that I'll use if I need to."

"I still don't... Wait, where did you get the daggers?" he demanded.

"If you don't want people touching your blades, you shouldn't hang them on your walls, Nico. Did you really think I was going to be dumb enough to do this without a weapon on me?" Sophia asked. He was glaring, but she knew he was also a little impressed. "You focus on getting a boat, and I'll meet you down near the tavern."

Nico let go of her arm. "Please, Sophia, don't run again."

"Have a little faith, Nicolo," she said, patting his cheek. Nico caught her hand and kissed the inside of her wrist.

"Go on, get out of here," he said, voice rough.

Sophia smiled at him. "Trust me, Nico. I'm not done with you either."

She adjusted the basket on her hip and walked calmly towards the soldiers, Nico's eyes burning into her back the entire way. She fixed her smile on the first soldier that spotted her. It was her time to shine.

CHAPTER SIXTEEN

Sophia held the basket close to her and tried to act humble. It was hard for a cocky pirate king not to stride straight up to the guards and kill them both. She had thought about it as an option, but she didn't want the entire garrison up her ass if they caused too much noise. Nico was going to find a boat, and it was her job to get the inventor and his daughter to the water.

"Good evening, sirs. I'm here to do the night clean," Sophia said, keeping her eyes downcast.

"What happened to Katja?" one guard asked gruffly.

"She was unwell and asked me to fill in for her," Sophia said, not looking up. "I'm a hard worker, sir. I will—"

"Sure, fine. Go on in," he replied, opening the gate for her.

Sophia hurried through the gardens to the back door to the laundry and kitchen areas. She spotted another three guards on patrol around the gardens. They all seemed bored and relaxed, smoking cigarettes and talking about sweethearts back home.

Maybe the inventor wasn't the troublemaking type, and they didn't have to worry about him running away? Frederico Orsini was a small, round-faced man with thinning hair who had given

Sophia no trouble the whole time she had been kidnapping him. His teenage daughter, Maria, had told them they would all burn in hell. She was her genius father's keeper from what Sophia could tell. She would have to find Maria first and get her to convince him to come willingly. Without her help, Frederico would keep writing his calculations and be lost in his own little world.

In the kitchen, Sophia abandoned the basket. She arranged a plate of grapes, cheese, and bread and poured some port wine. She shotted it and poured another. She hoped Nico was okay and hadn't been arrested already from asking dumb questions of the wrong people.

He's safer than you are right now, idiot, she reminded herself. She was discovering that she didn't like him out of her sight for long. It made the beast inside of her uneasy. Sophia thought it was pathetic, considering he was still angry with her. Her wrist burned where he had kissed it which reminded her that he might be coming around again. She couldn't think about kisses or anything they could mean. She had a job to do.

Sophia carried the plates, noting the two soldiers in the front of the house. They might be problematic. Sophia walked up the curving flight of stairs. She heard a woman singing and followed the sound. She tapped on the door. It was yanked open.

"What?" Maria demanded. Her eyes went wide. "You!"

"Shut up! I'm here to help," Sophia said, pushing her way into the room. "Keep your voice down unless you want your Varangian keepers up our asses."

Maria's eyes flared with rage. "What are you doing here?"

"Isn't obvious? I'm busting you and your dad out of here," Sophia said, putting down her decoy plates of supper.

"You sold us to them and now you are stealing us again? What the fuck is the matter with you?" Maria demanded in an angry whisper.

"If you remember correctly, I was going to sell you to the Venetian Navy. The Varangians were Kyrios's idea, and I couldn't stop it unless I wanted a sword in the gut." Sophia took a deep breath and tried to calm down. "You're pissed and have every right to be, but I really am trying to make things right again. At this moment, Nico D'Argento himself is stealing us a boat to get you and your father out of here, so work with me, Maria. Help me help you. I promise you can yell at me later."

"Fine. Let me get my shoes on. I hope you have a plan, pirate, because these guards are utter assholes." Maria pulled on a pair of boots. Sophia had to hand it to her—she was brave.

"We need to get your father. You lead the way," Sophia told her.

Maria didn't hesitate as she left the room and strode down the hallways. "He might be reluctant to move at this time of night. He's in a routine already," Maria said, like that explained everything. Sophia didn't care if they had to carry him between them; they only had a few hours to get out.

"What made you have a change of heart?" Maria asked her.

"The Republic is coming, and I want to make sure you two are both safe and out of the way before they get here," Sophia whispered back. "We need to hustle your father any way we can."

"Let me handle it," Maria said and opened the door. "Papa? You still awake in here?"

Sophia followed her inside the cluttered room. The inventor sat at a desk, piles of papers scattered around him. Calculations were scrawled over the walls in pen, like he was using them as a chalkboard. The Varangians clearly didn't care if he trashed the place as long as he was working.

Frederico was hunched over a notebook, writing furiously and muttering to himself. He hadn't even looked up when they came in.

"Papa? Sophia is here to take us to Venice at last," Maria said softly, resting a hand on her father's arm. He stopped scribbling and looked up, his owl eyes blinking.

"What was that, my love?" he said, focusing on her.

"We are going to go to Venice. Come now, let's get your coat on."

"Venice? At this time of night? What about the ships? Only five of them are finished."

"They are going to be fine. They want you to move on to Venice for a different project."

The inventor seemed to be hesitating, like he knew something was wrong, but his brain wasn't making the right connections.

"Arkon, the Grand Sorcerer, has sent me personally to retrieve you, *signore*. He said he has some new magio-mathematical problem for you to solve. Very complex. He can't do it himself," Sophia said, taking a stab in the dark at what might interest him.

"That sounds like him. Seventh son of a seventh son, did you know? I am too. We think a bit differently than others. Too many dimensions at once," he said with a little laugh. Maria helped him into his coat and shoes. Frederico picked up his notebook, holding on to it like a child would a favorite teddy bear.

"Do you need anything else?" Sophia asked looking at the piles of organized chaos around her.

"Oh, no, I have it safe in the vault," he said, tapping her temple. "Do you think Arkon will know anything about—"

"I'm sure he will," Maria insisted, cutting her father off. Sophia suddenly saw her perfect distraction and knocked a nearby candelabra over. The papers on the floor went up, the curtains to the room catching immediately.

Maria took her father's hand and nodded at Sophia. "We are ready."

"Follow my lead and keep up," she said. They hurried down the halls and almost crashed into two soldiers.

"Oh, sirs! Help! There is a fire in the inventor's room! The villa is on fire," Sophia cried hysterically.

"Fuck! Get them outside. If anything happens to him, we are all dead," the soldier said, shoving them aside.

Sophia took the old man's other arm, and they ran down the stairs.

"Fire! The villa is on fire! Help!" she shouted as loud as she could. Soldiers began running in from outside to see what was going on. Sophia went out the back kitchen doors and into the gardens. The other side of the villa was blazing, smoke pouring out of the upstairs windows.

"What the fuck has happened?" the guard asked. She recognized him as the one who had let her in the gate earlier.

"I don't know, but we were told to tell you to go and help them! They said something about saving the plans for the boats," Sophia said, fat tears in her eyes. "I do hope they are all okay."

"Goddamn it. Stay here and don't move," he growled out. He ran towards the house, disappearing inside.

"You missed one," Maria whispered, pointing to the lone guard by the gate.

"Look the other way," Sophia said, meaningfully. Maria nodded and turned to her father.

"Papa? Do you know the name of this tree over here?" she asked, pointing in the other direction.

"That? It looks like a lemon tree," Frederico replied, going for a closer look.

Sophia pulled out the two daggers she had stolen from Nico. Clearing her mind, she let a low whistle.

"What's—" the guard demanded just as the first dagger went into his throat. He clutched at it, gurgling blood before the second one went into his chest. Sophia caught him as he fell, shoving him back into the hedge and out of sight. She pulled the daggers out and swiped the blood off onto the man's jacket before sheathing them.

Maria already had her father to the gate. Sophia didn't look her in the eye as she opened it and checked the streets.

"Stay close to me," she said, and they ran through the gates and ducked into the alleys behind the houses. Sophia's adrenaline was pumping through her, coating her tongue in bitterness and making her heart race.

She needed to find Nico before...too late. Alarms were sounding behind them, but she didn't know if they were from the fire or that they realized the inventor was gone. Sophia slid to a stop at the end of a side street and pulled Maria and Frederico into the shadows. Four Varangians raced on without a second glance in their direction.

"I really hope you know where we are going," Maria whispered.

"The far end of the docks."

Sophia and Nico had agreed to meet near the small fishing docks near Blago's tavern. She knew he wouldn't let her down. Sophia's serpent side was thrashing urgently to get back to him.

I'm trying. I'm trying. Leave me alone if you aren't going to be helpful. Energy surged through her, and something tugged hard at her chest. What the hell was happening now?

Sophia grabbed Frederico's hand again, and they ran from house to house, keeping away from the main streets that were now crawling with soldiers. Blago's tavern had been emptied and locked up. Sophia cursed softly. He had taken her warning to heart and acted quickly. Unless she picked a lock, she couldn't hide in there.

"You, there! Stop right now!" a voice commanded. They stopped and turned. A Varangian soldier was coming towards them with a lantern. Sophia reached for her daggers, but before he could attack them, the man's head jerked hard to one side, and he was flung across the street.

"Stop to have tea, did you, sea rat?" Nico demanded.

Sophia smiled brightly at him, relief coursing through her like a drug. "Nice to see you too, honey. Did you find us a boat?"

"Yes, this way." Nico glanced at Maria and Frederico. "Pleasure to meet you both finally."

"And it's a pleasure to meet you too," Maria stammered, awkwardly staring up at him.

Sophia knew the feeling. Nico looked gallant and rakish in the moonlight, making Sophia think sexy thoughts. She kept a dagger out and held it low, but the docks were eerily empty.

"Where did everyone go?" she whispered to Nico.

"As soon as the alarms sounded, they all took off like they had rehearsed it. Come on, we can wonder about it later," Nico said, leading them down to the very end of the docks. There was a small boat with a mast already up and waiting.

"Watch your step, *signore*," Nico said, all but lifting the small man into the boat, followed by Maria.

"Here! They are over here!" a voice shouted. Nico held out his hand to her. "Come on, Sophia!"

"You won't make it without a distraction," she said, her body going into autopilot. She untied the boat and tossed the rope to Nico.

"Don't! Get back here," he said, reaching for the edge of the dock.

"Go now, Nico! I'll lose them, I promise. Get them to safety while you can."

"Fuck! Here, take this." Nico tossed the saint medallion at her. "I'll find you first."

Sophia caught it and tucked it into her bra. Heavy boots were thundering down the wooden planks. Sophia turned to the Varangians closing in on her.

"Catch me if you can, assholes!" she shouted and started running. Sophia could hear them panting and swearing behind her. She knocked over carts and small stalls that people had abandoned for the night. She just needed to lose them before she cut through the farms and got out of town.

She tore past Blago's tavern and slid in behind a house when something collided with her back, and she went sprawling onto the street.

"I got her!" a man shouted.

Sophia drove her elbow up into his nose as he tried to pin her. He swore, clutching at his face, and she managed to wriggle out from under him. She got to her feet and was instantly knocked down again.

"Lights out, bitch," a voice said. Pain shot through her temple, and she blacked out before she hit the ground.

CHAPTER SEVENTEEN

L eaving Sophia in Rogotin was the hardest thing Nico
had to do in his entire life. Frederico and Maria were
sitting at the front of the small boat with Nico at the
tiller. He didn't look back. He *couldn't* because if he did, he
would abandon the very people he'd been there to rescue.

The wind was good, so they made it back to where Savio
was hiding the *Reitia*. Arkon and Zahir were still aboard and
using illusion magic to disguise the huge warship as a merchant
vessel. Sophia had told them how to do it, and how it so easily
fooled Nico. A pang hit him in the chest. He wanted his troublemaker back.

"What went wrong?" Zahir asked, helping Nico up the rest of
the ladder and on deck.

"She... She stayed behind to distract the soldiers," he said,
voice rough. Arkon was already talking animatedly with Frederico and his daughter and ensuring they weren't hurt.

"Where're Dom and Stella?" Nico asked.

"I took them back to Venice to report to Gio," Zahir replied.
He shut his eyes briefly before opening them again. "You gave
her the tracking talisman?"

Nico nodded, a lump back in his throat. "She said she would follow us."

Zahir gave him an understanding look and patted him on the shoulder. Arkon joined them and realized what was wrong. "Where is the delightful Sophia?" he asked.

"Decided to be a distraction." Zahir glanced over to the inventor and his daughter. "How long do we wait for the pirate?"

Nico's hands balled into fists, and he stared across the water to where the river mouth was. They were just off the shore from Trpanj and a short sail for one of the Varangians' new warships. He didn't doubt Arkon's illusion work, but they couldn't wait forever.

"I can't leave her," he said through gritted teeth.

"You might have to," Arkon replied.

Nico's jaw clenched and unclenched. "You don't understand. I physically *can't* abandon my mate. If she's not here by dawn, I'm going back for her."

Arkon pinched the bridge of his nose. "And this is why mating shifters need to be relieved of their fucking duties."

"Don't be an ass, Arkon. It's not like Nico planned it," Zahir said softly. "I'll take the inventor and his daughter back to Venice. Nico can follow when he has Sophia. Arkon? Are you coming?"

The sorcerer looked at Nico and threw his hands up in the air. "Of course I'm not coming! I have to help Nico save his bloody pirate, don't I? If we go back to get her, the Varangians are bound to put up a fight, and Nico will need the help."

"You're a prick but also a good friend, Arkon," Nico said and hugged him. Arkon struggled against it.

"Stop it! Go back to be the glaring serpent prince we know and love. I don't know who this soppy shifter is," the sorcerer complained, pushing him away.

Zahir laughed softly. "Stop pretending you hate affection,

habibi. We all know it's a lie. Give me one moment, Nicolo, and I will trace Sophia for you." Zahir closed his eyes and glowing orange magic emanated from him. His eyes moved behind their lids, and he gasped.

"Shit," the djinn muttered, his eyes opening. "She's in a cell. They got her."

"Sophia is good at getting out of cells," Nico said, the words tasting bitter on his tongue. "I'll give her until dawn, but then I'm going to get her."

* * *

BY THE TIME the sky began to lighten two hours later, Nico was prowling up and down the decks. Zahir had gone, and Arkon was doing his best to fleece Savio at cards.

"Enough," Nico whispered, staring towards Rogotin. He was done waiting. Nico went into his cabin and dressed in his proper uniform for the first time in days. He knew his saber would probably be taken as soon as he stepped foot in the town, so he didn't bother taking any weapons. He trimmed his stubble and braided his long hair back into something presentable.

His eyes were glowing with his serpent. *Mate. Get mate. Now.*

"I'm going. We had to give her a chance. Sophia is better at escape plans than we are," he told it.

Nico tried his best to not think about whatever they were putting her through. It would only enrage him more, and he needed to have a clear head. He would get her back and then demand what she had been thinking running off and sacrificing her freedom. It had been the wrong time for her to decide to try and be noble. *Fuck.*

He felt the absence of her like she was missing a limb. They hadn't mated officially, and she was already a part of him. He felt like a damn fool for not telling her and for holding her at arm's length for the past few days.

What if the Varangians executed her? He would never kiss the path of her sweet little freckles or have her fight with him again. And he loved to fight with her. It made his heart race and feel alive.

Arkon was waiting for him when Nico finally emerged from the cabin's bathroom.

"Do you actually have a plan?" the sorcerer asked him.

Nico nodded. "Go to the town. Offer myself in her place. Get her back to safety."

"You'll be arrested, you big idiot."

"Not for long. I'll find a way to fight my way out or convince them to ransom me back to the Republic. I won't leave her in their hands, Arkon. Not when we were the ones that pushed her to try and rescue the inventor in the first place."

Arkon fished about in his pockets and tossed him a silver cigarette lighter. "Here, take this with you."

Nico caught the lighter. "And what am I supposed to do with this? Also, since when did you start smoking?"

"It's my good luck charm." Arkon grinned like a fiend. "Don't open it unless you want a really big distraction."

Nico had the sudden urge to drop it. "What does it do?"

"Can't you let it be a surprise? If you need such a distraction, open the lid and throw it," Arkon said, and his smile widened.

"It's a bomb?"

"In a manner. Just make sure you run once you throw it."

Nico put it in his pocket. "Thank you, Arkon. I'm sorry—"

"Don't," Arkon said, holding up his hand. "You need your mate. She's a devious one, and I'm sure the Republic can find a use for someone of her skills. Try not to die, okay? It would really inconvenience me to have to deal with recruiting a new council member."

"I promise I'll do my best," Nico replied with a smile.

Nico walked out on deck, nodding to the few soldiers that

were already up on their rounds. Savio was waiting for him by the ladder.

"Are you sure you want to go through with this yourself, commander? I could negotiate her release," he said.

Nico patted him on the shoulder. "I appreciate the offer, but no. This is my mess to clean up. Get the boat ready to sail. If I'm not back by midday, head for Venice. I'll find you."

"Please be careful," Savio said, and then his frown turned into a grin. "I would hate to have to keep this lovely ship for myself if you died."

Nico laughed. "Sure you would. Oh, and stop playing cards with Arkon if you want to have any money left at all. He's a terrible cheat."

"I am not. I'm a very good cheat," Arkon said coming up behind him. "Go on, go get your girl."

Nico climbed back down into the boat he had stolen and pulled away from the *Reitia*. On its small mast, he raised a white flag of truce and hoped that the Varangians wouldn't decide to shoot him before he made it to shore.

They didn't fire, but Nico did have a welcome party waiting at the docks when he sailed his little boat right up to the fortress that sat on the water.

I'm coming, Sophia. He hoped she was okay because if anything had happened to her... He didn't know what his serpent might do.

"I am Commander Nicolo D'Argento," Nico said, getting out of the boat and climbing onto the private dock. He raised his hands. "I'm unarmed."

"What is your business?" one of the soldiers asked.

"I wish to speak with General Leonid Siderov," Nico replied.

"In regard to?"

"That is a private matter between the general and me," Nico said. The soldier grunted and waved him on. He was surrounded in a moment, but they didn't move to cuff or restrain him. Nico kept his hands where they could see them. None of them was carrying guns, but that wasn't unusual. Magic made them unreliable, and the ones who weren't affected by it were too expensive for grunt soldiers. Cannons though? Cannons worked just fine. Arkon had tried to explain to him the mechanics of it before, something about the cannons' sizes negating the effects that caused normal firearms to explode. Most of the lecture had gone over Nico's head.

Nico was making note of all the cannons within the fortress as he was led through the heavy gates and up a wide flight of stairs leading to the battlements. He was glad he decided not to sail the *Reitia* any closer to land.

A table had been spread out with breakfast, and an imposing man sat at it. He was dressed in the charcoal and silver uniforms of the Emperor of Varangia and had an impressive curling moustache.

"When my men said that the famous Silver Serpent was sailing into our harbor, I almost had them whipped for attempting such a joke, and yet here you are," General Siderov said and gestured to the chair opposite him. Nicolo inclined his head and sat down. "I don't suppose you are here to change sides?"

"Unfortunately, no. I'm here about one of your prisoners," Nico replied.

"You will have to be more specific. I have quite a few rotting beneath us." The general's eyes narrowed. "Why would a decorated war hero come to bargain for the life of any of those scumbags?"

Nico took a steadying breath. "I'm afraid it's a family matter. The poor girl isn't right in the head and decided to come and get a closer look at the scary Varangian soldiers. I would like her back. She has red hair and was arrested in the wee hours of this morning."

"Your intel is very good," Siderov said with a small smile. He pointed across the water. "What do you think of my new ships? Big bastards, aren't they?"

"Indeed. They look like they will be impressive once they are finished," Nico replied.

Siderov nodded. "They will be. You have come to bargain for this woman, D'Argento, though you haven't offered anything in return. She stole something very important from me, and I'm inclined to kill her for it."

"That would be a mistake," Nico replied, levelling him with his coldest glare. "But you are right. If you give me the girl, I am willing to give Varangia back the mage it decided to send into Venice. He's currently very uncomfortable in the doge's cells. I can have him returned to you."

Siderov gestured to one of the soldiers. "Bring us the girl."

Nico knew Arkon would probably try and kill him for offering to trade the mage. He would deal with that once he got Sophia back.

"I swear to the dark gods of the sea I will bite your face off if you touch my ass one more time!" Sophia shouted as she was marched up the stairs. She stopped snarling when she spotted him. "Well, fuck."

"Ah, my crazy niece," Nico said, giving her a stern look. She had a busted lip and a broken nose, and the bruises around her eyes were already beginning to bloom. Nico swallowed hard. He was going to kill every person in that damn fortress.

"Uncle," she said between gritted teeth. "What brings you here?"

"Be quiet, girl. You have caused me enough problems," Nico snapped before turning back to Siderov.

"You really want her back? She has such a mouth on her. The women in Varangia are much more polite," the general said.

"Unfortunately, family is family. You understand. Let's settle this as gentlemen. Give her to me, and I will get the mage back to you," Nico replied.

Siderov smiled, revealing three golden teeth. "Why would I want the mage when I can have you, commander?"

"You would attack me under a flag of truce?" Nico asked, his eyes widening. There were some rules that were not to be broken, especially in times of war.

"You can see my predicament. I would be risking my honor as a general to attack you under a truce, but I risk my emperor's wrath if I let you go," Siderov said, spreading his hands before him. "Arkadi's wrath is something to behold, and I'm currently in favor with him."

"A predicament indeed. Honor lasts longer, and is much harder to get back than favor," Nico replied. He slid his hand slowly into his pocket.

"Nico! Don't even think about dealing with this flapping asshole! You aren't trading your life for mine. I won't allow it!" Sophia shouted, struggling against the soldier holding her by the shoulders. They hadn't manacled her wrists which was lazy of them.

"You're not in a position to bargain, sea rat," Nico replied, and her eyes went soft at the pet name.

"You utter bastard," she snapped. "How dare you put this on my head! I won't let you die for me."

"I don't intend on either of us dying today. Now, drop!" Nico said. In one quick move, he flipped the table, knocking the general backward in his chair. Nico pulled out the lighter, opened it, and tossed it towards the soldiers behind Sophia. She ducked down as a fire storm ripped free of the silver lighter, an inferno of bone-melting heat blasting over them. The soldiers screamed in fright and pain.

Nico smashed the chair into the soldier that was struggling to hold onto Sophia.

"What the fuck was that!" she screamed at him.

"No time," Nico said, tossing her over his shoulder and

running towards the watchtower. He cleared the doorway and hurried up the winding stairs.

"Wrong way!" Sophia complained from somewhere near his lower back. Nico dropped her to the stairs and disarmed the soldier coming down to meet them. He tossed him at the soldiers coming up behind them. Sophia was back on her feet and running. They reached the top of the tower, and she whirled on him.

"Now what, genius? We are trapped," she snarled. Nico pulled her close as soldiers swarmed up the stairs.

"Now, my beautiful mate, you hold your breath," he said and jumped off the tower. Sophia screamed in terror, but Nico was shifting before they hit the water. His serpent exploded out of him as Sophia scrambled to the surface and gasped in air. Above them, soldiers with cross bows were taking aim.

"I'm going to kill you!" she screamed, swimming towards him.

"Hold," Nico commanded through his fangs, and she scrambled up his neck to hang on to one of his horns.

"Swim fast, you crazy bastard! They are readying the cannons," she said, smacking him on the head.

"Hold your breath," Nico growled and dived under the waves.

He counted a minute in his head, his powerful body shooting out of the river mouth and into the sea. He breached the surface, and Sophia coughed.

Nico stayed above the surface, his serpent cutting through the waves until they made it back to the *Reitia*. He shifted back into his human form and grabbed Sophia.

"I'm… I'm hurt…" she gasped.

"Hold on. We are almost there," he said, swimming them to the ladder. He lifted her out of the water so Savio could lean down and pull her up. It was then that he saw the arrow bolts in her back.

"Careful, Savio! She's been hit." Nico was hauled up, and he scrambled to where Sophia was lying face down on the deck.

"Get the fucking med-mage and get this ship moving!" he commanded.

"You came for me," she wheezed, her eyes going blurry.

"No one gets to kill you but me, pirate," Nico said, picking her up and carrying her to the cabin.

"You...asshole," she said before her eyes slid shut.

CHAPTER EIGHTEEN

Sophia felt like she had been hit by a ship. The first thing she saw when she opened her eyes was a serpent battle in a stormy sea. She blinked rapidly, her eyes travelling over the painted frescoes above her.

She was lying in the middle of a large bed, buried deep in soft blue sheets. There were French doors that were opened to let in the soft sea breeze through gossamer curtains.

Sophia sat up with a wince. Where the fuck was she? Bells began to chime, and her stomach dropped. She walked on unsteady feet to the small balcony and saw familiar terracotta tile roofs and blue canals.

"Shit, I'm home," she whispered.

How the hell was she back in Venice? She stumbled over to the bathroom and tried to remember what the last thing that happened was. Fire and a tower came to her mind.

"Nico," she whispered.

Nico had come for her. He had been talking to the Varangian general who had made such a mess of her nose. She touched it tentatively. There was no pain.

In the mirror, she checked for bruising, but her body felt fine. She lifted up the men's shirt she was wearing and slowly turned around. Three fresh pink scars decorated her back. She sucked in a tight breath. She had been shot trying to get away.

Having the shit kicked out of her in the Varangians' cells had been bad, but nothing had compared to seeing Nico in his commander uniform, bargaining his life for hers. She had never felt so angry or frantic in her entire life. She had told him in detail what they would do to him and still he'd tried it. To save her.

She splashed water on her face and brushed her teeth. Someone had expected her to be awake because there were fresh toiletries for her to use and a robe placed on the end of her bed. She pulled it on and was immediately enclosed in the smell of sea salt and woodsy male aftershave.

"Nico," she whispered, burying her nose into his collar and inhaling deep. Longing mixed with anger once more.

She couldn't believe he had come for her. A part of her knew it was romantic in its way, but the bigger part wanted to chew him out for being so reckless with his life. He was the Venetian Navy's silver prince for fuck's sake.

Sophia opened the doors to the bedroom and went to find her idiotic mate.

No, not my mate, she tried to correct the voice inside of her.

Mate, it repeated. She rolled her eyes. It wasn't going to listen to her, but she knew better. Look where she was! This wasn't a life she could ever be a part of. Sophia walked out into a hall with beautiful paintings in heavy gold frames and the D'Argento family portraits. The floor was the fancy red and white speckled marble that Sophia could never remember the name of, except only rich people had it.

"Ah, you are awake," an older woman said, coming up a sweeping staircase. She was dressed in an elegant black silk suit, and Sophia's insides shriveled. General Josefina D'Argento was a tall woman with the same commanding presence as her nephew.

"Um, hello, general," she replied, feeling naked in Nico's robe. She hadn't even brushed her hair, just charged out on a mission to find him.

"I'm happy to see you up. Nicolo has been quite insufferable to be around for the last two days," she said. She looked Sophia over. "So you are the Pirate King."

"I was," Sophia replied, meeting her gaze. She wouldn't be intimidated by Nico, and she wouldn't be intimidated by his aunt.

Josefina surprised her by laughing. "He's on the second-floor balcony, eating lunch. Go easy on him."

"He tried to hand himself over to the goddamn Varangians! He'll be lucky if I don't toss his ass into the nearest canal," Sophia said, her temper flaring again.

"Oh, dear. You two really are suited for each other. I'm going to make myself scarce for the next few days. Try not to break anything too expensive," Josefina said, shooting her a wink before she went on her way.

Sophia blinked rapidly. That...was not how she thought a conversation with the general would go. Sophia shook off her stupor and went down the soft velvet covered stairs.

The palazzo was ridiculous. If she did decide to rob it, she would need three ships to carry the contents. The concept of old family homes was foreign to her, but she could tell that someone had made changes recently.

For a start, of all the portraits of gallant looking D'Argentos, there wasn't a single one of Nicolo's father. Nico hadn't been exaggerating when he said how much he hated him.

After another ten minutes of exploring, Sophia found the commander sitting in the sun at a table, reading a paper. Her heart did a ridiculous tango as she let her eyes roam over him. He was dressed in comfortable looking clothes, his hair in a messy knot. It was the most casual she had ever seen him. God, he really was a handsome beast of a man. The Venetian light loved him, turning his tan skin golden.

Mate, the voice said, softly this time.

Shut up. He's not for us. Though Sophia didn't know if she believed that anymore either. Her stomach growled loudly, and the moment was ruined. Nico looked up, his blue eyes zeroing in on her. Sophia swallowed hard, trying to remember what she had been about to say to him.

"Come and eat, Sophia," Nico said.

"Don't tell me what to do, "she replied and then felt like an idiot.

"You've been asleep for two days and had med-mages healing you around the clock." Nico's gaze went cold. "You will come and eat something, or I will make you."

"God, can you not be a dick for five seconds?" she huffed, walking over to him. He pushed the chair out beside him with his long, bare foot. Sophia sat down and drank the glass of juice in front of her.

"Did Maria and Frederico get out okay?" she asked before inhaling a croissant. She was starving.

"They are well and are guests of the doge," Nico replied. His eyes traveled over her, making her want to climb under the table and hide. "How are you feeling?"

"I'm fine. Just hungry," she swallowed a mouthful of fruit. "And once I'm finished eating, I will be pissed, so prepare yourself."

Nico's mouth ticked in one corner. "I'm quivering with fear, sea rat."

"You're going to be," she grumbled before starting on the pile of bacon. She couldn't remember the last time she had eaten.

Sophia did her best to focus on the view of the blue canal and the boats drifting through them. It wasn't that she didn't love Venice. She did. She just didn't know if she had a place there anymore. She finished her coffee and turned on him.

"You are never going to do something so stupid again," she said, trying to keep her anger out of her tone.

"You'll have to be more specific. There has been a lot of stupid in the past week," Nico replied, putting down his paper.

Sophia's hands fisted. "Coming after me and trying to deal with that fucker of a general was a dumb thing to do, Nico."

"He was going to execute you," he said, eyes icy again.

"Maybe, but maybe not? I'm a fucking *pirate*, Nico. I knew what that entailed when I signed up for it." Sophia took a deep breath, but it didn't help. "You are worth more alive. This city, the Republic, your aunt. You have things to live for. They all need you."

"And I need you," he said, voice so soft, she wasn't sure she heard him right.

"Did you hit your head when you jumped off that stupid tower? No one needs someone like me." Sophia got to her feet, needing to move before she exploded.

"You know you could say thank you for rescuing you," he said, standing up to face her.

"I'm never going to say thank you when you do something so reckless! You should have left me behind and gotten yourself to safety like I told you to."

Nico loomed over her, but she refused to back down. Her heart was beating too fast. A trickle of sweat slid behind her knees, and she didn't know what to do about any of it.

"You aren't my captain," Nico said, getting in her face. "You are my goddamn mate, and I will *never* leave you behind."

"I am not your fucking mate! Get it through your big serpent head."

"Yes, you are, and I'm going to prove it." Nico grabbed her and kissed her roughly. Sophia pulled him to her, her whole body singing with happiness. She delighted in the rightness of being in his arms and having him dominate her with his perfect mouth and hard hands.

Sophia's common sense kicked in, and she pulled back, untangling herself from him. "That was nice, but it doesn't prove anything."

"You're a damn liar. Your serpent knows the truth. Maybe you should listen," he said.

Sophia began to back away from him, and his blue eyes went gold. "It was hell for me to let you go, and I won't be doing it again. I would've torn that fortress down brick by brick and burned Rogotin to the ground to get to you."

"Stop this nonsense. You're not thinking clearly," she said, still backing away as he followed.

"No shit I'm not thinking clearly. My mate is right in front of me. She almost died, and now she won't stop saying she's not my mate," he replied, all growl. "I'm *done* playing this game with you, Sophia. You're mine, and you need to accept it."

Sophia's body flooded with adrenaline, her flight instincts kicking in and telling her to get out of there as fast as she could.

Nico's smile went feral, and her pussy clenched in excitement. Holy goddess of the sea, she was not okay in the head. He was a monster, and she had never wanted something more in her life. No, no, no.

"Thinking of running? Go right ahead," he taunted, nodding to the open door on the other side of the room. "But I hope you studied the house plans well when you planned to rob me because if you run, I will chase, and I will fuck you where you fall. Or you can sit down again, and we can talk this through like adults. Those are your only options. Your choice, *dolcezza*."

A dark thrill swept through Sophia, desire and danger

mixing together and making her blood sing. She knew he wasn't fully in control of himself, and the serpent side of her wanted to rile him until he lost all of his gentlemanly manners. Feral Nico was her favorite Nico.

Sophia ran.

CHAPTER NINETEEN

Sophia bolted down the hallway, Nico hot on her heels. She slid around one corner, knocking over a pedestal with some kind of fancy vase on it. Nico didn't stop to catch it. It smashed to the marble floor, and he leaped over it.

Sophia squealed and headed for the stairs, taking two at a time. She went through another open doorway, blindly looking for a way through as she pulled another chair behind her to slow him down.

Sophia yanked open a door that led into a study with books and a big globe. She looked left and right and was reaching for another door when Nico barreled into her. Sophia hit the soft oriental rug, air knocking out of her in a whoosh as the big shifter landed on top of her. She squirmed, red faced and trapped.

"Should have studied those house plans a little better," Nico purred in her ear. Sophia could feel his hard dick already pressing into her ass, and she groaned. Hot lips brushed over the back of her neck. "You know what happens now, don't you, my naughty mate?"

"Nico," she whimpered. She knew he would stop if she asked,

no matter how lost he was in the game. She didn't want him to stop; she wanted him inside of her, filling her up and making her feel alive.

Nico's big hands slid up her bare thighs and dragged the fabric of her shirt up. He made a small growl of satisfaction before his lips pressed into her lower back over a fresh scar.

"In the past two days I think I've lost a decade of my life worrying about you," he admitted against her skin.

"You have?" she whispered.

Nico pressed his face into the curve of her spine. "Yes. A few times there, I thought I had lost you. *Never* do that to me again, Sophia."

Her heart ached at the pain in his voice. Did he really care that much? It was so strange to have someone genuinely give a shit about her that she didn't know how to process it.

"You missed me bad, huh?" she teased, her breath catching when he nipped her skin softly.

"Far more than I thought possible."

Sophia bit her lip to keep herself from smiling. "Prove it."

Nico didn't hesitate. He pulled the shirt off over her head and proceeded to cover her neck and back in maddeningly soft caresses and kisses.

"I'm going to take my serpents and kill every last one of those Varangians for hurting you," he promised her. "Especially the fucker that broke your ribs."

"I had broken ribs?" she asked. Everything had happened in a blur.

"Two broken ribs, a broken nose, a busted lip, three cross bow bolts, and a sprained ankle," Nico counted off. "I've been losing my mind for days, waiting for you to heal and wake up."

"You have very good med-mages," Sophia replied, swallowing hard. She had no idea she had been so hurt. Everything was a haze of pain and darkness.

Nico hummed against her. "Nothing but the best mages for my mate."

"I don't think I'm your...fuckkk," she moaned as Nico stroked his fingers over her pussy.

"Oh, my Sophia, there's no fucking doubt you are my mate. You're so fucking wet for me right now," he said, plunging a finger into her. Sophia gasped, her hips lifting higher to give him room.

Nico chuckled softly. "That's what I thought, *dolcezza*. Mine. *My* mate, *my* sweet little pussy to fuck whenever I want it."

Sophia hated that he was right. Hated and loved it, because she couldn't get enough of him and how he made her feel. "For a rich boy, you sure have a dirty mouth."

"It's the company I've been keeping lately," Nico said and added another finger. The stretch felt so damn good, she thrust back against him. He had her pinned and unable to move, and it was exactly what she needed, what she wanted.

Nico's free hand stroked up her back and buried into her hair. "Look at me."

Sophia turned her head, and his lips crashed down on hers. He bit her bottom lip, making her gasp and open for him. His tongue moved against hers, his heat and taste flooding her senses. She was losing her mind with every deep stroke of his fingers, his mouth so hot and commanding.

"Come for me. I want you good and soaked," he said, his eyes going golden.

"Oh, gods."

Nico's mouth twisted in a little smug smile before he slid his thumb over her clit and she was coming apart, stars dancing in front of her eyes.

"Hmm, so you *can* obey orders in the right circumstances," Nico said, going in for another kiss that scorched her to the bone. He pulled back and ran his thumb over her wet bottom lip. "Now, I will fuck you boneless."

"H-Here on the floor?"

"I told you what would happen if you ran," he said, his hand tightening in her hair until her scalp tingled deliciously. "And I'm a man of my word." Nico thrust his dick into her with one stroke, making Sophia swear at the deep slide and stretch.

"Fuck, Nico," she gasped when he hit her limit over and over. This wasn't just fucking; he was claiming his territory. It was the only battle she decided she was happy to lose. It didn't matter if she thought a future with him was impossible. All that mattered was that he wanted her despite it all.

"You are so damn beautiful," he groaned, his hand dipping under her to squeeze her breast. "I want you so much, you drive me fucking crazy, every goddamn day."

"You love it," she panted. Nico pulled out of her and flipped her onto her back. He lifted her up and thrust back into her, making her grab on to his strong forearms. His body rippled with muscle and flushed brown skin as he moved inside of her.

"I do love it," he admitted, his fierce face hovering above hers. "And I will make you mine, Sophia. I don't care how long it takes. I will have you."

Sophia pulled him back to her mouth. "You big idiot, I'm already yours."

Nico cupped her face with his hands and kissed her deeply. And then with a wicked smile, he fucked her until she was screaming her way through another orgasm. Only Nico could make her lose her fucking mind so completely. He buried his face in her neck as he came, dragging his teeth down her skin in a way that had her coming all over again.

He braced himself on his forearms, careful of his weight crushing her, and stroked the curves of her face.

"I love your freckles," he admitted and kissed their pattern across her cheeks.

Sophia burned red at the unexpected sweetness. "Whose office is this?" she asked, a bubble of laughter rising up in her.

Nico grinned. "It's mine, and now it's going to smell like fucking for months."

"A good thing you're always at sea," she replied and tried to move. Nico slid off her, and she felt like she would float away at the sudden lightness. His eyes had gone back to a melting sapphire color, and she didn't fight him as he scooped her up off the floor. She rested her cheek against his chest and listened to his heart thundering.

"Thank you for coming to get me," she said softly.

Nico kissed the top of her head. "I told you on that ridiculous little island you ran away to, there's nowhere you can go where I won't follow you."

Sophia kissed the curve of his collarbone. "Psycho."

"You keep pretending you don't like that about me," he replied. He took her back to the room she'd woken up in and into the bathroom. He set her down on her feet before turning on the shower and pulling her into it.

"You do realize this palazzo is ridiculous," she said, staring about at all the pretty gray marble around her.

"It's a lot, but it is the family home," he replied with a small shrug. "I haven't been here enough in the past few years to make any changes."

"Except to get rid of all the portraits of your father."

Nico wiped the water from his face. "You noticed that? As soon as his funeral was over, I tossed every painting of him into the canal."

"And I used to think you were the stuck-up prince who never did anything bad," Sophia chuckled and kissed his wet chest.

"I don't know where you got such a ridiculous notion," he replied, lifting her chin so he could kiss her. "Now that I have you all sweet and relaxed, I need you to know that I meant what I said about you being my mate."

Sophia rested her forehead against him and groaned. "Nico,

be realistic. I can never be your mate."

"I want to know what makes you believe that," he replied. He took some of the soap from the dish and began to wash her in gentle strokes. "Explain it to me, Sophia. I'm trying to be reasonable."

Sophia gestured at the insane bathroom. "Look around you! I don't belong in a place like this. I was a bastard, born of a chorus girl, and then I became a pirate for fuck's sake. What makes you think I would be a good mate to someone like you?"

"You commanded a ship full of pirates, Sophia. You became their king. You can handle dealing with a few servants to cook and clean for you. You don't like the house? Change it. I don't care. I just want you in it."

Sophia huffed out a breath. "I'm not the type of woman who would be happy being locked up in a pretty house, waiting for her man to come home from sea. I grew up on the docks and saw that all the damn time."

"I never said I wanted you to do that. You've met Stella. She's a human and mated to someone as equally as powerful as I am. Do you think she sits at home and idles away, waiting for Dom? You can be whatever you want, Sophia. Just...be mine too," Nico said with a shy smile. "You know the goddess doesn't make mistakes when it comes to mates. Reitia knows you are the perfect woman for me, and so do I."

Sophia struggled against all the voices in her and the memory of all those scornful looks she got when she was a poor girl fishing down at the docks. The way her mother had longed for her rich lover to come and take them out of the poverty that haunted them. She had barely dared to look anyone rich in the eye back then. And now she had the Silver Serpent himself wanting her to be his mate.

"It's going to take me a little bit to wrap my head around all of this, Nico. I wanted to kill you less than a fortnight ago. It's a big change," she said, trying her best to be honest. "Can you give me a little time to figure out what I'm going to do now?"

Nico pulled her close. "I already told you. I'll wait until you get used to the idea. No running from me. That's all I ask."

"Okay, no running. Well, unless you want me to run," she said, trying not to grin when his grip on her tightened. "So what are we going to do about those fancy Varangian ships?"

"We?" Nico asked, earning a jab in the ribs.

"Yes, we. I'm not letting you go back there alone, and we can't let Siderov have enough time to finish building the other ships."

Nico sighed. "I know we can't. We have been summoned to meet with the Council this afternoon to discuss what to do about it."

"I'm sure you'll have a great time," Sophia said. "I'll stay here and eat cake in bed."

"Oh, no. Your presence has been requested specifically. I've been holding them off since we got back to Venice, but I received the official summons this morning, demanding we both be there." Nico grinned down at her. "Gio wants to meet you."

Sophia's grip tightened on him. "Nico, I can't meet the doge."

"Scared?" he asked and waggled his brows.

"No, but he's the *doge*." She was absolutely scared. He could overturn Nico's deal and hang her off the side of the balcony.

Nico's laughter echoed around the polished marble. "You called the Emperor of Varangia's personal general a flapping asshole to his face, and you're scared of Gio? You can't be serious."

Sophia pushed him half-heartedly. "Fine! I'll meet him, but I'm not responsible if it all goes to hell and I embarrass you."

"You won't." Nico only brought her close and kissed her until she forgot all about what she was meant to be mad about.

CHAPTER TWENTY

Nico wanted to stay in bed with Sophia. He didn't want to go and sit in the council chambers and go over everything that had happened in Rogotin. He already knew it had been reckless and out of character for him, but seeing Sophia roaming about the palazzo and making fun of his ancestors made it all worth it.

Stella arrived at three o'clock with bags of clothes and other mysterious feminine things he had no business knowing about. He had sent a bag of money over to her that morning, asking for help, and she had more than delivered.

"You are looking a lot calmer than last time I saw you, *amico*," she said with a teasing smile.

"She's safe, and that's all that matters." Nico shifted his weight. "I don't suppose you could convince her to be my mate? She still doesn't believe me."

Stella patted his arm. "She knows, Nico. She told me. She's just scared at the possibility of it. Give her some time."

"I'll give her until the Varangian ships are destroyed," he replied gruffly. Stella only laughed at him and poured herself another wine. They both knew he would wait forever.

Sophia had known all along that Nico was her mate. Of course she did. Nico ran a hand over his face. He couldn't think about it now, but when the meeting was done, they were going to have words.

"How pissed do you think the council is going to be?" Nico asked her. He straightened the cuffs of his uniform and checked the time. They had thirty minutes to get to the palace and Sophia still hadn't emerged.

"You know what they are like. They will bitch about your actions on one hand and forget all about it because you and Sophia got the inventor out of there," Stella replied. She had sat through enough council meetings to know how the game was played.

"Are you two ready?" Sophia asked, finally coming downstairs.

"*Mio Dio,*" Nico whispered, his heart stopping. Sophia was dressed in a sapphire blue suit and a black silk camisole with a lacy trim. She wore heeled boots, her red hair pinned up in a loose, pretty style. Her green eyes were lined in kohl, and her lips were a deep burgundy. Nico forgot all about the council meeting and instantly wanted to get those red lips around his dick.

"Well, don't you clean up well, commander," Sophia purred and flicked one of the silver epaulets on his shoulder. "You're just asking to be fucked in this uniform, aren't you?"

"Yes. I don't want to go to the meeting anymore," he said. He really wanted to toss her over his shoulder and go back upstairs.

Sophia put her hands on her hips. "It's too bad. I put make-up on, Nico. We are going to meet the fucking doge."

"You heard the lady," Stella said, clapping her hands to get them moving.

They were close enough to walk to the palace, but Nico knew if he did, he would be stopped too many times with people wanting to say hello. They got into Stella's boat, and she drove them the short distance to the council members' private docks. Sophia was looking about her with an expression Nico couldn't decipher.

"Are you okay?" he whispered.

"I'll be fine. This is... I just feel weird being here with you," she admitted.

"Get used to it, sea rat." Nico helped her and Stella out of the boat, and as a group, they headed for the guarded palace doors. A cart was selling gelato to children at the waterfront, and Sophia tugged on his hand.

"Can we get some after?" she asked.

Nico smiled at the sudden burst of unguarded sweetness on her face. "Of course we can. I'll buy you a tub of it if we can get through this meeting without bloodshed."

Sophia screwed up her nose. "What if it's not our blood?"

Nico tried not to laugh. "Get moving, you troublemaker."

Arkon was waiting for them outside of the council chambers. He was slouching against the dark wood paneling, looking like he'd rather be anywhere but there. Nico knew the feeling.

"Ah, here you two are! I was starting to think I'd had to drag you away from your game of 'climb the mast' myself," he huffed, straightening up.

"Try not to sound too jealous," Sophia said.

Arkon rolled his eyes. "You wouldn't even be here if it wasn't for my med-mage skills, so check the attitude, pirate."

"That was you?" she said.

"I told you, only the best for my mate," Nico replied.

Arkon put an arm around Sophia's shoulders. "I stayed behind to help get you out of Rogotin out of the goodness of my heart."

"Bullshit. You want something, sorcerer," Sophia said, raising a brow. "Spit it out."

Nico knocked Arkon's hand off Sophia's shoulders. "No touching."

"Don't be like that. Sophia is my friend," Arkon chided him. He was wearing a shit stirring grin that told Nico the little bastard knew exactly what he was doing.

The door to the council chambers opened, and Dom appeared. "We are ready for you lot."

Nico rubbed Sophia's lower back where no one could see. "I won't let anything happen to you."

"Promise?"

"I promise." Nico leaned down to whisper in her ear. "Just think of all the gold you were promised."

"And the crown," Sophia whispered.

"I would never forget the crown." In fact, Nico had a specific one in mind.

Inside, the rest of the council members were in their usual seats. Zahir smiled at them, and Aunt Josefina gave him a small wink.

Nico hid a proud grin. Josefina supported his mating like she had supported him with everything else. She was the closest thing he had to a true parent, and her approval meant more to him than he could articulate. He had thought that the general in her would be furious that his mate was a notorious pirate, but she had only laughed when he had told her.

The Great Hunt, as Zahir had called it, compelled mates to do strange things. Like piss of an entire Republic to get Nico to come after her.

He knew Sophia was nervous but only because he knew her tells. She wore a guarded, almost bored expression on her face as Arkon introduced her to the rest of the council. She executed a perfect bow to Gio.

"It is an honor to meet you Doge Loredan," she said with such deep respect, Nico almost believed it.

"Is it? After causing so much chaos, I've been led to believe you had no interest or respect in the Republic," Gio replied.

Sophia raised her head and fixed a knockout smile on her face. Nico's breath actually caught.

"Then, with respect, your intel has been lacking. If I hated the Republic so much, I wouldn't have risked my life to save the inventor and his daughter. I also wouldn't have a great plan to deal with the remaining ships and get information out of the Varangian mage locked in your cells," Sophia said, as sweet and serene as Nico had ever seen her. Who was this woman? She'd never mentioned the mage. Nico never could seem to figure out what she would do next...and it thrilled him.

"We look forward to hearing those plans, *signorina* Osara. Please take a seat," Gio said, and she sat beside Nico. Under the table, her fingers tangled with his, and he tried not to let his happiness spread out all over his face. He was sure that Arkon would've told Gio about Sophia being his mate. They might disagree at times, but they were tighter than friends, and Gio was the only person that Arkon would listen to.

Nico told the council of his official deal with Sophia, the rescue of Frederico and Maria, and Sophia staying behind so they could get away. He didn't exaggerate anything; she really was as impressive as she appeared. Nico couldn't leave such an asset behind. Gio asked questions about Siderov and their operation before turning to Sophia.

"I would like to hear your suggestion about how to handle these war ships," Gio said, gesturing to Sophia. "I want guarantees that you are willing to make up for past crimes."

Sophia didn't look repentant. It wasn't in her nature. She ignored that part of the question entirely.

"The islands along the coast are pirate territory. The Navy doesn't know how to navigate through them, where to hide ships, where latest wrecks are and so on," she began.

"But you do?" Lorenzo Tera, the representative from Coins interrupted.

"It's how I've managed to outrun, out-hide and generally

outsmart the Republic for the past two years. So yes, *signore*, I do know them well," Sophia replied. "You will need my help to guide Nico and his serpents through those waters. If you try and sail in with a fleet of ships as a frontal assault, the Varangians will form a blockade and sit in their fortress. If Nico goes in with cannons, the people in the town will suffer."

"Did they not side with the Varangians?" Lorenzo pressed.

Nico wanted to tell him to shut the fuck up and listen instead of interrupting.

Sophia's green eyes narrowed at Lorenzo, and every man and djinn at the table felt their balls shrivel. "The town is *occupied*. There was no 'siding' with anyone. When an army of Varangians rolled into town, there was no Republic to come to their aid. They chose not to die, but they aren't happy. If you do this without hurting innocents, you will get Rogotin back and cut off the Varangians from the coast once more."

"Sophia is right. We need to draw them out somehow. The town is a strategic asset we need," Arkon said, rubbing his chin. "If we don't bring in the navy, what's your thoughts?"

"The Varangians know Nico's boat. It will be like waving a red flag at a bull after he almost scorched Siderov's face off. They will want payback. I would take Nico's ship and fill it with the best serpents in Venice. We sail the hidden ways to Rogotin, drop the serpents in the water. The Varangians will think it's just Nico with his ship. When they sail out with their fancy new ships to turn the *Reitia* to splinters, the serpents will fu—ah, destroy them. Talk to Frederico, he will know the best place to hit the boats and how to do it for the most impact."

Gio grinned. "Take her, Nico. Make it happen. What was the idea you had about the mage?"

"With respect, doge, I would like to discuss that idea with Arkon first," Sophia replied. "We can present it to you once we hash it out."

"Very well. What's next on the agenda?" Gio said, and the meeting moved on to other topics.

No one had suggested that Sophia still be punished or objected to the deal Nico had made with her. It was a good thing because Nico really didn't know what he would do if her life was threatened again. He tightened his fingers around hers, determined to never let her go.

CHAPTER TWENTY-ONE

A s soon as Gio had dismissed them, Nico took Sophia's hand and tugged her through a doorway. "This way. I have something very important to show you before anyone tries to talk to us," he said, making her laugh.

"Are you going to show me where the doge's treasure room is?" she asked hopefully.

The palace had an abundance of secret nooks and store-rooms. Nico knew them all. He pulled Sophia into the nearest one, pinned her to the wall, and kissed her. She grabbed the stiff collar of his jacket and pulled him closer. Her lips were urgent and eager, meeting him head on as she usually did. She bit his bottom lip, making him groan.

"Do meetings always make you this horny?" she asked, pulling back from him.

"Only when you're beside me, giving out battle plans. Fuck, you're so damn perfect."

Sophia ran a hand over the bulge in his pants, her lipstick smeared smirk making him lose his mind. She reached over and locked the door. "We wouldn't want to get interrupted now, do we?"

Nico went to kiss her again, but she dodged it and pushed him back against the wall. His whole body tensed as she dropped to her knees.

"You have been asking for it all day, wearing this slutty uniform," Sophia said, undoing his belt and pants. "Really, you should be more careful about what you wear."

Nico groaned with the first soft, wet flick of her tongue. She smiled wickedly and deep throated him so fast, his head banged back against the wall in surprise. She came off him with a pop.

"Don't mess up my hair," she warned before sucking him down again. Nico couldn't breathe, didn't know what to hang on to as the heat and suction of her mouth made him lose his damn mind.

"Look at me," he managed to gasp out. He stroked her face before sliding his hand down to grip the side of her throat. "Let me know if I need to stop." She nodded, and he began to thrust faster, fucking the perfect heat of her. He watched as her hand slipped inside of her own pants, and he wanted to strip her bare so he could watch her play with her pussy for him.

Nico's orgasm danced, tingling down his spine, and as he tried to pull out, Sophia sucked on him harder.

"You better swallow all of me, or there will be trouble," he warned her, pumping into her another two more times before he was coming harder than he had in his life. Sophia moaned around him, lost in her own release.

Nico wiped the tears off her cheeks and pulled free from her when he got too sensitive. He lifted up off the floor and pulled her hand from her pants.

"That's mine," he growled and sucked the sweetness from her fingers.

Sophia's eyes were hazy from lust, and it was a look he loved best. He kissed her, the taste of them both sending his serpent mad with wanting her.

A heavy hand knocked on the door, startling them both.

"Hurry the fuck up, you two!" Arkon shouted through the door. "I know you're in there."

Sophia giggled. "Oh my god, put me down and help me get the lipstick off my chin."

Nico gave her his clean handkerchief and tucked himself back in his pants. She fixed her lipstick before wiping the red off his own mouth. Once everything was in order, Nico opened the door and found Arkon waiting a little further down the hall. The sorcerer turned and pointed at Sophia. "You missed a spot," he said.

Sophia looked down at the dusty patches on her knees and laughed. "Shit. Thanks." She brushed her pants down. "You would think the storerooms in the doge's palace would be cleaner."

"Their dirtiness matches the council members, it would seem. Honestly, you could have waited," Arkon said, but he was grinning.

"And what's so urgent you felt the need to interrupt?" Nico asked, already thinking of the fastest ways to get Sophia home.

"Your beloved here suggested an attack on the Varangians, or did that piece of information slip your mind?" Arkon said, crossing his arms. "We are going to Zahir's to plan things in more detail because we are leaving Venice tomorrow."

"Why Zahir's?" Nico asked, his brain muddled from Sophia sucking all of his thinking power out through his dick.

"Because the inventor is with Ezra, and he will know the best places for the serpents to smash the ships. Really, Nico, you need to focus."

"Yeah, Nico," Sophia added with a small grin.

"Don't you start," he warned, and she only smiled wider.

"You two are pathetic. If you can put aside your animal mating instincts for a few hours and focus on the task at hand, we would all appreciate it," Arkon huffed and began walking off. They followed him outside into the failing afternoon light.

"Wait, I'll be right back," Nico said and hurried over to get Sophia her tub of gelato.

"We have a battle to plan, and you're worried about ice cream?" Arkon demanded.

"I keep my promises," Nico said and handed Sophia the tub. She went misty-eyed for a few seconds before quickly looking away.

"Anything else or can we leave?" Arkon pointed at Sophia. "You better be sharing that."

They walked to Cannaregio where Zahir had set up house with Ezra. Arkon always used shielding magic for getting around the city, so Nico knew there was no way they would get recognized. Dom and Stella were already there, pouring wine and chatting. Ezra lit up when she saw them come through the front door.

"Here they are!" she called and hurried over for introductions. "Frederico has been telling me about you coming to rescue him. It sounds like I've missed all the fun."

Zahir slid an arm about his consort's waist. "You've had enough excitement lately."

"He worries like an old woman," Ezra said before her welcoming expression chilled. "But Sophia, if you do anything to hurt my djinn again, I'll fuck you up."

"Noted, and I apologize for my part in that. As I told Zahir, I'd never cross the djinn, and if that Varangian had told me what he had planned, there is no way I would have agreed to it," Sophia replied and then added sincerely, "I really am sorry."

Ezra's expression warmed once more. "I accept. Now let's move on. I want to hear all about your plan to take down these ships Frederico has been telling me about."

"And I still haven't forgotten we need to talk about your plan regarding the mage," Arkon added to Sophia. "What's rattling around that head of yours, pirate?"

"Oh, all kinds of trouble," Sophia replied, and Nico believed it. He idly wondered if she had an idea at all, or if she was just bluffing her way through it. He never could tell.

Sophia waited for the others to head further into the house before rising up on her tiptoes and kissing him sweetly on the cheek.

"Thank you for the gelato."

Nico's heart swelled, and he brushed a thumb over her lips. "You're welcome, sea rat. Now, let's go plan a battle."

"You really do know how to turn a girl's head, D'Argento," she said, and her smile was all pirate.

CHAPTER TWENTY-TWO

I t was midnight by the time they got home to Castello. They had a plan, and Nico had sent out summons to have the serpents meet the follow day at the *Reitia* for their mission. His aunt would stay behind to protect Venice with Zahir acting in Arkon's usual position. Nico had voiced concerns about bringing him along, but Zahir had taken him aside.

"Arkon needs a release or he's going to snap. I don't want him in Venice when that happens," Zahir had told him. "You can't feel the pressure of his magic, but I can. Point him at something and let him blow it up for all of our sakes."

Dom and Stella were also joining them. It was going to be strange to have so many friends in a battle, but their plan was sound, and he couldn't talk them out of it. Besides, he had a different kind of battle to wage that night.

"Why did I think heeled boots were a good idea?" Sophia said, kicking them off as soon as she was through the door. "I don't suppose I could convince you to carry me upstairs?"

Nico sighed like he didn't love that she asked and hoisted her in his arms in a bridal carry.

"Now that I have you so you can't run away, I want to know all about how you told Stella I was your mate because you keep telling me that you're not," he said, tightening his grip.

Sophia became a wriggly explosion of arms and legs, but he held on and carried her the rest of the way to his bedroom. Nico set her down, and she instantly started stripping.

"I have a better idea than talking," Sophia said. Nico had to admit, it was distracting, but he wasn't going to be happy until he got it out of her. He played along, taking off his heavy military jacket and watching as she lay on his bed completely naked. He rolled up the sleeves of his shirt. If this was how she wanted to play, he would be happy to oblige her.

Nico grabbed her by the ankle and tugged her down to the sheets toward him.

"You are still wearing too many clothes," Sophia complained. Nico smiled and then lightly bit the inside of her wrist. Her lashes fluttered, and he almost gave in. Nico kissed the delicate curve of her collarbone.

"Tell me why you have been lying to me, Sophia," he growled softly against her skin.

"I haven't been lying," she lied again. Nico sucked on her nipple hard, making her gasp and squirm. His hands stroked over her skin.

"You knew I was your mate the first time we were together. That was why you ran to that silly little island, wasn't it?" Nico asked.

"Maybe?"

That whole escapade was suddenly making a lot more sense.

"Did your serpent wake up and tell you that I was your mate?" Nico cupped her other breast, kneading it softly.

"Yes, but I'm not about to listen to some random part of myself that has never bothered with me before. It's not...real," she replied.

Nico stilled his exploration. "You think I have no say in what my serpent wants?" he asked.

Sophia propped herself up on her elbows. "You are a serpent. I'm just half of one. Of course you don't have a say in what your serpent wants. It's why I have to be the clearheaded one of the two of us," she argued.

Nico shook his head. "It's not how it works, *dolcezza*. Yes, the mating instincts will make you do some strange things, but if the rest of me wasn't on board, I wouldn't be here right now." He placed a gentle kiss on the curve of her stomach. "I would want you even if you weren't my mate."

"I don't know if I can believe that," she replied, her fingers stroking through his hair.

"That's okay. I'm willing to keep proving it to you." He spread her legs wider to accommodate him. "You're my mate. You know it in your bones, and you're going to admit it to me."

"No, I'm not," she said, unconvincingly. She was maddening.

"Yes, you will. I'm going to make you tell me all those dark little thoughts you have in your head about us and why you believe that we can't be together," Nico said, pressing a kiss to the curve of her hip.

"You're going to use sexy torture on me? You beast."

Nico bit the back of her knee. "You knew this about me. I can always stop, and we can have a proper conversation? No? I didn't think so."

Sophia made sweet, helpless sounds as he kissed his way back up her inner thigh. His serpent tracked every movement and moan, lingering whenever a flush lit up her skin. He would make her believe they were perfect for each other if it was the last thing he did.

"Tell me why you don't want to be my mate, Sophia," he said, his mouth hovering over her pussy.

"Because we aren't suited," she said stubbornly.

Nico licked her, relishing the sweet taste of her. She was already so wet, and he had barely touched her.

"Lie," he replied. He swirled the tip of his tongue over her clit before pulling back. "We both are not so secret psychos, as you eloquently put it. We love the sea. We love to fight. We definitely love to fuck."

Sophia's back curved up, her breasts rising up in a way that had him reaching for them again. She was so small and curvy compared to him. All that softness matched and molded to his hardness. Nico licked her again in a lazy stroke.

"All of that...isn't what matters," she gasped. "I can't be what you need."

"And what is it that you think I need?" Nico only needed her. He slid a finger inside of her, stroking the warm heat until she was gasping.

"Oh god, you're a terrible person," she complained.

"You can make me stop at any moment. Now answer my question, and I'll let you come." Nico curved his finger inside of her, brushing against her G-spot in the way that she liked before stopping again.

"*Basta*! You need someone that can be the serpent princess, okay? I'm not highborn. I can't do fancy. I don't know how. I feel weird being in this house with you. Like I won't ever belong. You will get tired of playing 'fuck the pirate', and I'll end up sad and heartbroken just like my mother!" she shouted.

Nico stopped teasing her. He stopped everything. He climbed up on the bed next to her and cupped her cheek. Her eyes were filled with unshed tears, and it made him feel like he'd been kicked between the legs.

"Hey, look at me," he said softly, turning her head. "I'm not your piece of shit father. I've been paraded about like some kind of prize for all those highborn ladies as you call them, and I've never once thought they would be a good match for me. I don't have to be anything I'm not with you. You see me. The real me.

AMY KUIVALAINEN

All of the bad. And you're still here. That means more to me than you being my mate or an exciting time. You know me to my core, Sophia, and I've never felt that way with anyone. Not even my own family. It's why I love you so much."

Her green eyes went wide. "You... You love me? What about all the annoying things I've done to you in the last few months? I tried to kill you like a week ago! I ran away a bunch of times—"

"Doesn't matter. If anything, it kind of made me love you more. Everyone sees me as the Silver Serpent or the commander. They aren't game enough to call me on my bullshit or make me fight for them. You do. You don't really give a fuck about the palazzo or the money. None of it impresses you. *Mio Dio*, I'm offering it to you on a plate and you still don't want it," Nico said, a small laugh escaping him. "You are going to challenge me every day of my life, and that makes me feel...alive."

Sophia sniffed. "How can I not love you when you say stuff like that?"

Nico saw the minute she gave in, and then she was kissing him like she couldn't get enough.

"If you hurt me, I really will hang you from my mast."

Nico tucked a loose curl behind her ear. "You don't have a ship anymore."

"I'd take the *Reitia* as revenge," she said, climbing on top of him.

"That's fair. It's also never going to happen. I'm a serpent, *dolcezza*. We are worse than dragons. I don't toss my treasures away," he replied, sitting up. She pulled his shirt off and he kicked off his pants.

"Let's talk about this some more after we defeat our enemies tomorrow," she said and kissed him. "Tonight, I just want to fuck you senseless without any worries about the future."

"I'd like that," Nico said and tucked his hands behind his head. "Help yourself, my perfect mate."

Sophia's grin turned feral, her serpent turning her eyes gold.

Nico went impossibly harder. Sophia edged back and guided his dick to her pussy. Nico gripped on to the pillows behind his head as she used her wetness to slick him down.

"I've been thinking about getting you in me all damn day. How dare you turn me into such a needy beast?" she said, guiding him inside her.

"I regret nothing," he gasped.

Sophia moved with gentle thrusts until he was fully seated inside of her.

"Nico? Look at me," she purred, and he fixed his eyes on hers.

"Yes?"

"I love you too," she whispered. Before he could answer with anything sweet, she dug her sharp little nails into his chest and began to ride him.

All thoughts but the weight of her, the tight, wet heat gripping him, fled from his mind. She was glorious, her red hair catching the light and turning it to flames. His hands moved from her breasts to the swell of her hips.

His gorgeous mate. She was fire and desire and violence and madness. She was the best thing that could have ever happened to him. It didn't matter that she couldn't shift. She was pure alpha serpent, taking everything from him that she was owed. His heart was hers. Everything was hers.

Nico ran a thumb over her panting lips, and she sucked it into his mouth, making every part of him tighten.

"You better come soon, *dolcezza*. I don't know how much longer I can hold out while you do that," he warned her, his voice strained.

Sophia laughed and guided his wet thumb to her clit. "Then do your job, D'Argento."

Nico grabbed her ass, squeezing it roughly. "Oh, that's the game you want to play, is it?" He thrust up hard, making her gasp in surprise.

"Fuck baby, do that again," she begged.

Nico took over the pace, dragging her down on his cock and working her clit at the same time. Sophia's head went back in ecstasy as she clenched and came hot all over him.

Nico sat up and bit down into the beautiful column of her throat. The taste of her skin sent him over the edge, and he clutched her to him as he filled her up. They were both breathing heavily, their hearts beating next to each other.

"Mate," he growled, whisper soft.

Her arms went about his neck, and she whispered back. "Mate."

CHAPTER TWENTY-THREE

S ophia had never seen so many serpent shifters in one place before. Nico moved about the deck, greeting them all by name and giving them positions they would take in the upcoming battle.

He usually had ten shifters on board with him. He now had triple that amount, and the energy was erratic.

Sophia stayed at her position at the ship's wheel, Savio standing not far from her in case she needed anything.

Her own serpent was feeling more alive than ever. She had no urgency to try and shift, but she had access to a different kind of power that she never thought possible. It was like finding Nico had unlocked that hidden part of herself and she was now complete. With him close by, she wasn't just complete but content.

She had always been a roiling ball of restless energy, always rushing to the next thing that caught her attention. She always was chasing that next high. Nico had calmed that side of her, making her think sappy thoughts like maybe she had been hunting him all along.

"You seem quiet," Stella commented, coming up the stairs.

She was dressed much the same as Sophia—in pants, loose linen shirts that protected them from the sun, and flat-soled, knee-high boots. She carried beautiful daggers on her hips, and if Sophia hadn't liked her so much, she probably would have tried to steal one.

"I have a ship of shifters that know I'm a notorious pirate. It seems prudent not to be a wise ass," Sophia said, keeping her grip light on the wheel.

"That hasn't stopped you before," Savio commented.

"Savio, you really need to stop acting like you don't like me. It will give a girl a complex," Sophia replied. He gave her a thoughtful look and then shot his middle finger at her. Sophia roared with laughter, making Savio grin. "Ah, I knew you had a sense of humor under there somewhere."

Stella came to stand beside her. She was shuffling a well-used deck of tarot cards in her hands.

"Tempting Fate?" Sophia asked her.

"What? Oh, no. Shuffling helps keep my hands busy, that's all. You're welcome to one," she said, fanning them out for her.

Sophia had loved her deck that had gone down with her ship. She reached for a card and then pulled her hand back.

"No, I can't do it. I don't want it to mess with my brain before going into a fight," Sophia said, looking back out at the ocean.

"And you don't want to know about Nico?" Stella teased.

"We've been using our words," Sophia replied. "Like adults."

"I'm glad to hear it. It's better you don't make a mistake by waiting too long." Stella looked across the far side of the deck at Dom.

"Sounds like a good story."

"I met him; we connected, and then I ghosted him for eight months because I was scared of who he was." She laughed softly. "I didn't think I could fit into his world."

"But you did?" Sophia pressed. "How?"

Stella shrugged. "We changed the world so it fit us instead."

Sophia chewed on that for a while. If Stella could make it work, she was sure she could too.

For now, Sophia had to focus on the next battle ahead of them, not the one that would come after it.

They were making excellent time. It was greatly attributed to Arkon and the other mages on deck who were filling the sails with the maximum amount of wind.

They had left Venice at dawn. Sophia hadn't slept much thanks to her need to have Nico fuck every worry from her body. It was going to be a long day, followed by a longer night.

The plan was to get to Rogotin by midnight. They would have Arkon cause a fuss and then get the ships to come after them.

Nico had gotten everything he needed from Frederico in regards to the ships' weak points and had been busy sharing that information with his small army of serpents. They were valuable enough that only a handful usually sailed with each ship in the navy. The *Reitia* had the most on an average day. Today was not average, and the destruction they could cause with thirty of them? It both frightened and thrilled Sophia just thinking about it.

"I've never been in a battle before," Stella admitted.

Sophia tried to hide her surprise. "Really? And you chose *this* madness to bust your battle cherry?"

Stella laughed. "We haven't been ready before now. My magic needed training, which Arkon has helped me with. I think he wants this to be a big fuck you to the Varangians, and having Dom and I here will help with that."

"How's that? What are you two going to do?" Sophia asked.

"You will have to wait and see," Stella replied and waggled her brows. "We want it to be a surprise."

That just made Sophia even more curious. Arkon saw them

talking and walked from the front of the ship to join them. He *looked* like the Grand Sorcerer for once.

Sophia didn't know him well, but he seemed to be a man of many faces. Today, it was his imperious war face. He was in head to toe black with an impressive coat embroidered with the golden winged lion of Venice on its back. Underneath the lion was some kind of sigil that shimmered strangely if Sophia looked at it too long. His curls were wild about his face, and there was a fuck you glint in his eyes.

"Feeling okay, sorcerer?" she asked as he joined them.

"Ready to cause some chaos. Where are we?" he asked, staring about.

"Not far from Split. We are going to be in position by dusk if we keep up this pace. I've never seen a ship move so fast," Sophia commented.

She had been at the wheel all day, wound up and alert for changes in the tides and always on the lookout for pirates. Her old companions had no doubt heard of the Varangians attacking her ship before the crew was picked up by the *Reitia*. They had always been smart enough to steer clear of Nico. It was only Sophia who had been that reckless.

Her eyes shifted from the horizon to where Nico was standing and found him watching her back. She tried not to smile at him. He was engaged in serious business, but all she wanted to do was kiss him.

"Eyes on the horizon, captain," Arkon teased. "You can make heart eyes at Nico after the fight."

"Stop being such a spoilsport."

"You can use this excellent opportunity to explain your plan regarding the mage," Arkon pressed.

"That's easy. Put me in the cells with him," Sophia said, adjusting their course to avoid the sandbar she knew was lurking ahead.

"I don't think Nico will agree to that."

"Which is why I'm telling *you* this plan and not him," she replied. "I can convince the mage that I was hired to bust him out. He knows for a fact I can get in and out of Venice."

Arkon rubbed at his beard. "And what is this meant to accomplish?"

"He'll tell me whatever I want to know to get him out of there. You want to know if the Wolf Mage really had a falling-out with Arkadi? He might know. He had military connections. He was always bragging about them," Sophia explained. "I'm kind of surprised you haven't gotten everything you needed out of him."

"He has this strange block in his mind. It was made with magic. It's a fail-safe of sorts. Without going into boring detail, it makes it so the information can't be tortured out. It needs to be freely given. And he will never freely give me anything," Arkon replied, his frustration written into the frown line between his brows.

He was handsome but strange to look at because he was caught between ages. He couldn't have been older than forty, but his hair and stubble were streaked with silver. When he wasn't playing about, his eyes looked ancient. He was someone that had been blessed with too much magic and responsibility too young.

Sophia had seen her brother age quickly too for similar reasons. Tito had been a mature man at fifteen.

"I can get it out of him, Arkon. I can be really convincing when I want to be. Let me give it a shot at least," Sophia said, her eyes going to Nico again. "If I'm getting forced to go legit, I need to have something to occupy myself with. My skill set is not hosting garden parties and acting like a princess."

Stella and Arkon shared a look before he turned back to Sophia.

"I can't recruit you as a raven. Nico would actually kill me, but I can maybe make you an honorary one to help me with projects that utilize your special skills," he said, and she smiled.

"I'd like that. I want to be with Nico, but I need something to keep me busy."

Arkon smiled, and it wasn't sarcastic for once. "You suit him, you know?"

"Yeah, I know," Sophia said. Her body still throbbed with the delicious memory of him pounding that fact into her the night before.

Nico loved her, and she believed him. She would just have to hang on to it on the days that she felt awkward being the D'Argento mate. She had known in her soul that she wouldn't walk away from him and that she wasn't capable of letting him go. The thought of him being with anyone else filled her with a maniacal kind of rage. That was how she really knew she was in love.

The sun was dipping below the water line when Nico finally came to stand beside her.

"How are you feeling?" he asked. "You've been at this wheel all day."

"I'm looking forward to getting this battle done so you can take me home and teach me how to be a pampered princess," she replied, smiling up at him. He was still in commander mode, so she resisted kissing him, but gods, did she want to.

The ship slowed as they reached the coast of the small island of Hvar. It was a short sail to Rogotin, and it kept them hidden from anyone looking for ships.

"After tonight, I will have earned a short vacation with my mate. We still need to make it official, and when I do, I'm not going to let you leave my bed for days," Nico whispered to her. Goose bumps broke out over her arms at the heat in his voice. He looked at her like he had last night—like she was something worth having. Like he wanted to possess her and keep her safe. It ruined every thought in her brain.

Sophia bit her lip and quickly turned away from him, her breath catching in her chest. "Get your serpents ready. We attack in an hour."

"Yes, sir," he purred, and she almost came.

"That was mean."

"Punish me later?"

Sophia laughed. "Oh, that's a promise, commander."

CHAPTER TWENTY-FOUR

Excitement curled in Sophia's belly. She had never seen the serpents fight before, and she watched them dive from the boats and get into position.

"Are you ready?" Arkon asked, positively vibrating. Sophia could feel the magic locked tight around him.

"Try not to blow yourself up," Nico said, brows drawing together in concern for his friend.

"Good advice for you to follow," Sophia said, walking across the deck to the diving platform.

"Would you miss me?" Nico teased.

Sophia sniffed and looked him over. "I would certainly miss parts of you."

"Be careful with my ship," Nico said, leaning down until his lips almost brushed hers. "Or there will be trouble."

"You got me scared. Now, get going," she said, moving back from him before she embarrassed him in front of his men.

"Fuck it," Nico grumbled and pulled her back to him. He gave her a hard kiss that scorched her insides before letting her go.

"Do I get a kiss goodbye too, or can we get on with it?"

Arkon asked, stepping between them. "Off with you, Nicolo. We don't have all night."

Nico gave Sophia one last look before diving overboard. She went to the side of the ship in time to see him shift to his serpent form.

"Okay, Arkon, get your ass in the dinghy," Sophia said, and the sorcerer climbed down the ladder. "Are you sure you can sail? I'd hate for you to tip and drown before I see any fireworks."

"I am Venetian! Of course I can sail!" Arkon called back, all ruffled indignation.

Sophia waited, watching as he sailed towards the Neretva River's mouth. She let him get a good distance before she signaled to the crew to get the *Reitia* following him.

Nico's serpents fell into formation behind the ship as Sophia guided them out of their hiding place. She spotted Nico's large head as it breached the surface, his gold eyes watching her.

"Gods of the deep, he's so big," she said, full of awe.

"Keep focused," Savio prompted her, but not unkindly.

"Are you sure you don't want to join them?"

Savio shook his head. "Nico trusted me with you and the ship. I just hope you're as good in a fight as the rumors claim."

"Try not to be jealous when you behold my magnificence," Sophia said and shot him a wink.

"Please let me know when that happens in case I miss it."

Sophia tossed her head back and laughed. "I won't have to tell you. You still have eyes on Arkon?"

Savio pointed. "He's in position, so we'll slow the ship. I don't trust he—"

Fire exploded out of Arkon, lighting up the dark night. A fire ball the side of a carriage hurtled over the water before hitting the watchtower.

"Holy shit, he's a human trebuchet," Sophia gasped.

Arkon wasn't satisfied with only one fire ball. He started to lob them one after the other, smashing into the half-built ships on the shoreline. Alarms and bells started ringing, carrying across the water. Two ships were already undocking and heading their way.

Arkon continued his barrage before the winged Venetian lion lit up like a firework. It raced across the night before eating a silver wolf.

"Subtle, he is not." Sophia laughed in wonder.

"That's our signal," Dom called and shifted into his shedu form. Sophia had always been jealous of the shifters with wings, but she still went across the deck to look at him.

"You're a big boy, aren't you?"

"The biggest," Stella said. She was dressed in dark red leather armor, her hair in a tight braid. She mounted onto Dom's back. "Wish us luck!"

They launched into the sky, and Sophia felt like she was about to witness history. She had no idea that shedu let anyone ride them or that Stella was such a badass.

The other three Varangian ships had left port, their speed already astounding as they charged through the water.

The first one was drawing near to Arkon's boat.

"They will run him down," Sophia said.

Savio grabbed her arm. "Wait, Stella has him."

Dom swooped down, and Stella was suddenly wreathed with crackling lightning.

"What in the gods..." Sophia gasped. Stella unleashed her lightning, striking the sails of the Varangian ship and sending the crew scuttling. Dom flew lower and grabbed Arkon in his paws seconds before the ram on the Varangians' ship plowed through the small boat.

Dom flew fast over the *Reitia* and dropped Arkon. The sorcerer hovered over the deck before lightly landing on his feet. His eyes glittered with power.

"Get the cannons ready. They are almost in range!" Savio commanded, and the crew got into position.

"Having fun, sorcerer?" Sophia called out.

Arkon's returning smile was one of the most terrifying things she'd ever seen.

"Get me closer," he called back, and Sophia turned the ship's wheel and headed straight for the oncoming ship. She was about to hit it with their ram when the Varangian ship shuddered like it had hit a reef. The hull was blown apart, and Sophia saw the glimpse of serpents' spines.

The Varangians started to go down, and Arkon lit up like their own personal stream of Greek fire. A whip like cord of flame burst from his outstretched hands, wrapped around the mast of the ship, and snapped it like a twig.

Soldiers were leaping off decks only to be met with the snapping fanged jaws of the serpents. A large tail wrapped around the back of the ship and tugged the wreckage under the waves.

"One down, four to go!" Sophia shouted, steering the *Reitia* away from the rubble in the waves.

The night was filled with the roar of serpents, the sky splitting with lightning every time Stella and Dom flew past. Arkon's magical flames lit up along the water, incinerating everything that they touched. Sophia's ears were ringing with cannon fire, and Savio was hoarse from shouting orders.

Still the battle raged, and none of them slowed or stopped. The serpents were engaged with Siderov's larger flagship, the Varangian harpoons firing into the water, wounding any serpents that got into range.

Sophia and Savio had the cannons firing volley after volley.

Arkon was fighting beside Sophia, his magic hot and pulsing around him. He froze, grabbing her arm.

"Something is wrong. I feel..."

He never got to finish. A sonic boom pulsed out of the front of Siderov's ship and through the water. The sea became a roiling mass of serpent bodies as they all writhed in panic and agony.

"They have fucking mages on board! We need to stop them," Arkon said.

Nico, Nico, Nico. She needed to find him.

Arkon gave her shoulder a hard shake. "Sophia, focus! I need you, and so does Nico."

"Okay, okay. Signal Stella. I'll swing the ship about to make another pass by. Dom can grab us and take us over there," Sophia replied.

Arkon shot up a flaming signal, and the golden shedu made their way towards them.

"I don't know if you should come," he said suddenly.

"I'm not asking your fucking permission. That weapon is hurting my mate!" she shouted at him.

"Take a few of these then. They are fire storms like the one I gave Nico," he said, passing over the square silver lighters.

Dom landed with a thump on deck, and Arkon hurried to tell them the plan.

Sophia grabbed Savio, pulling him aside. "The ship is yours."

Savio's lips pressed into a tight line. "Go and help them, Sophia. Please don't die."

"Aw, you do like me!" she said, kissing his cheek.

"You're growing on me," he replied gruffly.

Sophia hurried back to where Stella and Dom were waiting.

"Are you ready?" she asked, tiny bolts of static were dancing over her skin.

"As I'll ever be," Sophia said. She grabbed hold of Arkon, and Dom cradled the sorcerer in his massive paws.

"I fucking hate flying," Arkon grumbled.

"Think of all the fun we are going to have once we land," Sophia replied. She didn't hear his reply because as soon as Dom took off, there was nothing but the sound of wind roaring and cannons booming. Sophia gripped on to Arkon and sent a prayer to whatever god was listening that she wasn't going to be dropped into the sea or hit with a cannon ball.

Lightning crackled past Sophia in hot arcs, Stella unleashing herself on the crew of Siderov's ship. Once a space was clear, Dom dropped them. Sophia screamed into Arkon's chest as they plummeted downward.

Warm wind and magic wrapped around them, cushioning their fall and dropping them lightly to the deck.

Sophia had her saber and dagger out in seconds, ready to meet the first soldier that went for her. She kept her back to Arkon, and they cut through the Varangians swarming them. A mage threw a ball of water at Arkon, who caught it with a laugh and tossed it back, smashing it against the other man's face and knocking him out.

"Who the fuck is this guy now? Are Varangians breeding half-baked magic users?" he complained. Sophia looked over her shoulder at where the unfortunate mage was now wrapped in chains. How and where they came from, Sophia had no idea, but clearly Arkon had been hiding just how powerful he was for years.

A strange mechanical whirring sound caught Sophia's attention.

"Arkon! What the fuck is that?" she shouted. She fell into a quick fighting rhythm—slash, cut, dodge, lunge, block. Her serpent was roaring for blood, the fear for Nico and need for revenge stripping her of any pity for the soldiers coming at them in waves.

"Sophia! I've found the device! Firestorm!" Arkon shouted.

Sophia took one of the lighters from her pocket, flicked open the lid, and threw it at where the soldiers were coming out from below deck. The world went red hot and golden with fire around her, the soldiers cringing back and accidentally impaling themselves on the wave coming up behind them. Sophia stood guard in front of Arkon.

"The mage was generating this blasted device. It has a line into the water that—" he trailed off, pulling at something.

"That's great! We will take it with us! Focus, Arkon!" Sophia shouted at him. "What are we going to do now?"

"Now is the time for something very special. Be ready to jump from the ship when I say so," the sorcerer replied. He had the device wrapped in his coat. He pulled a black orb from his pocket.

"Arkon? What is that?"

The sorcerer gave her a wild smile of pure chaos. "I've been waiting to use this. Ready?"

"No, I'm not ready!" Sophia called, sheathing her saber.

Arkon let out a maniacal laugh, flung the sphere, and they jumped from the side of the ship. Sophia threw her dagger at the water, breaking the surface before she hit it feet first. She plunged into cold darkness.

A glow in the water had her whirling in time to see the world above the surface turn crimson. The shockwave sent her hurtling through the sea, and she kicked hard to get herself upright. She breached the surface with a gasp, desperately sucking in air.

"Arkon?!" she shouted, coughing out salt water as she searched. "Arkon!"

"Sophia, I'm here!" the sorcerer called, and she swam to him. "Well, that worked better than I thought."

There was nothing left of Siderov's ship. Not a piece of stray debris or a strand of rope. Sophia stared in awe and a healthy dose of fear at the sorcerer cackling with glee in the water beside her.

"You are a fucking lunatic," she said and started laughing too.

The serpents were dragging the last ship beneath the waves. It was over.

"Better send a signal to Savio to come and get us. I don't want to drown after surviving you, sorcerer."

Arkon shot up another flame, and the *Reitia* turned towards them. The crew dragged them, wet and exhausted, on board.

"Where is my mate!" an angry voice demanded from somewhere.

Sophia lay on the deck, too wet and tired to move. Nico loomed over her. He looked livid. Blood was running from his ears, and there was a wound on his shoulder. He had never looked so fucking good.

Sophia gave him a lazy smile. "Hello, lover. Did you have a good swim?"

Nico picked her up and squeezed her tight. "Yes. Apart from coming back just in time for Savio to tell me you were on Siderov's ship before it blew up." He kissed her deep and pressed his forehead to hers. "Everything is fine now."

CHAPTER TWENTY-FIVE

They went back to Venice the following day in a post battle daze. Three of the Republic's ships sailed in to take back the town of Rogotin and sort out what remained of the Varangian fortress.

Nico and Sophia had been in bed since they had returned home, and he had no intention of that changing until it needed to.

It had taken a full day for his ears to heal and his vertigo to go away. He thought he'd never feel pain so terrible again. That was until he saw Arkon's bomb completely blow up Siderov's ship. He was still furiously mad that he'd taken Sophia with him and used an untested weapon at the same time. Nico wasn't sure his heart was working properly yet.

He pressed a kiss to the top of Sophia's hair and slipped out of bed. Tossing on a robe, he walked through the villa to his office and unlocked the family safe. Inside were the deeds to his houses and rare and expensive jewels that had been passed down through the family.

After some digging, Nico pulled out an ebony wood box and cracked open the lid. He smiled and shut it again before locking the safe up. He had a pirate in the house after all, and one couldn't be too careful.

Nico went back to bed and found Sophia awake. She smiled sleepily at him, and he wondered how he'd gotten so lucky.

"What do you have there, handsome?" she asked with a yawn. "And why isn't it coffee for me, your beloved?"

Nico laughed and sat down on the bed beside her. "This is better than coffee."

Sophia pushed her hair out of her face and rolled so she could look up at him, flashing her naked breasts and making him forget what they were talking about.

"Nothing is better than coffee. You're clearly still delusional from having your bell rung so hard," she said and rubbed at her cheek. "So what is in the box?"

"It was going to be a mating present, but I decided I wanted you to have it now. I don't care how long you wait until you decide to make things official. I'm just...here," he said gruffly, his words failing him. He laid the box in her lap. "This is for you."

Sophia opened the box and let out a gasp. "Nico, I can't have this."

"Nonsense. I promised you a crown, didn't I?" he said.

"Well, if you insist." Sophia lifted the tiara out of the box, her eyes shining. It was made of twisting silver serpents and dark blue sapphires.

"It's a D'Argento heirloom, and it's now yours." He gently took it from her and placed it on her tumbled red curls. "There, and you said you weren't fit to be a princess."

Sophia launched herself at him, kissing him until he was breathless. "You're never going to get it off me now."

"I don't want it off you," Nico said, shrugging off his robe. "I want you to keep wearing it while I fuck you until you're screaming my name."

Sophia climbed into his lap, her clever hands finding his

already hard dick. "I mean, it *does* seem the polite thing to do when a handsome gentleman gives you a crown."

Nico bit her bottom lip hard, making her pupils blow out. "Oh, sea rat, I'm no gentleman."

Sophia let an excited meep sound as he flipped her over onto her hands and knees. She was naked except for the crown, and it was the sexiest thing Nico had ever seen.

"What are you waiting on?" she complained.

Nico gave her ass a hard smack, making her groan.

"I'm just admiring what belongs to me," he said, soothing the red mark with his tongue before spreading her and licking her wet pussy. He would never get enough of the taste and heat of her. She was battle and lust, and better than anything he'd ever dreamed of.

Nico played with her clit, making her whimper so sweetly that it almost undid him. He pressed two fingers inside of her, stretching her to accommodate him.

"Fuck, Nico, get inside me already," she begged.

"I'll fuck you when I want to and not a second before," he said and nipped the inside of her thigh. "You're not the captain here, remember?"

Nico couldn't make out what she said in reply. It was too muffled by the pillow she was biting into. He used her wetness to slick himself down before pressing the tip of his cock into her. Her back arched for him so prettily as he slid in, inch by inch.

She rose up on her forearms and threw him a sassy look over her shoulder. "Is that the best you got, D'Argento?"

Gods of the deep, this woman.

Nico thrust hard into her, making her slide forward with a startled moan.

"Fuck, yes, Nico, just like that," she urged, and his serpent lost it. Nico grabbed her by her hips and pounded deeply into her, her cries guiding him where she needed his dick the most.

She clenched hard around him, screaming out his name into the bed.

"Again," he grunted, one hand grasping around her slender throat, the other sliding over where they were joined and up to her clit. "I need you to come again."

Sophia turned her head to kiss the hard muscle of his forearm. "Nico, I accept you as my mate."

Nico's vision hazed, his instincts taking over his body at her surrender and acceptance. He pounded into her, needing something to help release the electric energy scorching his veins. He could sense the bond between them blowing wide open, and he could feel her serpent like it was a part of him.

"I accept you as my mate too, Sophia Osara," he managed to gasp out. Too much emotion was riding him as he moved deeper inside of her.

Fangs lengthened in his mouth, and just like she sensed it coming, Sophia offered him her throat. The sound that came out of Nico wasn't human as he bit into her sweet flesh, and he came so hard, he didn't know when it would end.

She was sobbing her way through her another orgasm, her pussy clenching around him as her body shook with tremors. Nico rolled onto his side, taking her with him and cradling her into the warm protection of his body. He was still inside of her, and nothing had felt so perfect.

"Mine. My beautiful mate," he whispered, his fingers brushing over the smooth skin of her hip.

"You're still not the boss of me," she replied before turning her head and giving him the sweetest kiss ever bestowed on a man before. "And I'm *still* going to get double my body weight in gold."

Nico laughed, his whole body shaking with the joy that rocked through him. "Always the pirate."

"And yet, you still love me."

Nico kissed her soft, sassy mouth. "I really do."

CHAPTER TWENTY-SIX

The following day Nico knew that he couldn't put off meeting with the council any longer. Sophia tried to get out of going, but she couldn't avoid it when a personal note arrived from Gio requesting her presence.

"You're lucky that I love you so much that I'm willing to suffer through it," Sophia said, tossing the note onto his desk. "Who does he think he is summoning me?"

"The doge?"

Sophia huffed. "Well, he's lucky he's so hot or I'd ignore him completely."

"What do you mean that he's hot?" Nico growled, but Sophia was already sailing out the door to go and get ready. She was such a diva when she wanted to be.

My diva pirate, his serpent grumbled.

Thirty minutes later they were in a boat and heading towards the palace. Nico hadn't heard from Arkon since the battle, and it seemed strange for the sorcerer to vanish.

"What are you frowning about?" Sophia asked, taking his hand once they arrived.

"Nothing. Worried about Arkon. He's too quiet. That makes

me nervous."

"He's probably still sleeping off his magic exhaustion. I'm sure he's fine," Sophia replied.

Nico was glad to see Arkon waiting for them outside the council chambers.

"Finally!" he said. The manic gleam he had in his eye from the battle hadn't left.

"Have...have you slept at all?" Sophia asked, taking note of his rumpled appearance. His usual stubble was more of a beard, and his curls were standing up at odd angles from where he'd been running his hands through them.

"I think so? I must have. A bit? I've been taking apart that sonic weapon we found, and I've made the strangest discovery," he said, beginning to pace.

"Tell me about it after the meeting," Nico replied. He had lost three serpents in the confusion and pain that the weapon had caused. They needed to find out not only how it worked, but how they could defend themselves against it.

Inside the meeting room sat the other council members apart from Josefina, who was still in Rogotin.

"Ah, the heroes of the hour," Gio commented as they sat down. "We are ready to hear a report. I tried to get information out of Arkon, but he's a little distracted to be coherent at the moment."

It wasn't said unkindly. Arkon was a genius sorcerer, and that came with its privileges and its trials. Even now, he was staring at the frescoes on the roof, his eyes totally glazed. Zahir was frowning at Arkon in concern and shot Nico a look that told him they would be taking care of the sorcerer that evening.

Between Dom, Nico, and Sophia, they recounted the entire battle and the aftermath. The other council members noted the need for a service for their soldiers who had died and proper compensation for their families.

"As for you, Sophia Osara, you are proving quite a valuable

asset, so I have a new mission for you," Gio said, leaning back in his chair.

"For me?" Sophia replied innocently. "I don't know what use I could be."

Gio smiled, like he knew she was trying to wriggle out of it. He wasn't a shifter, but Gio was as much of an alpha as Nico was. He also had been doge for seven years, and that was a feat within itself. He was no fool and could read a person quicker that anyone in the Republic.

"I have had a pardon drawn up for all pirates within the Adriatic. If they join the navy as privateers for the rest of the war, they will be forgiven for their crimes against the Republic," Gio replied. "You will take this offer to them as you are the only person who will know how to find the other captains that swore allegiance to you as their king."

Sophia bit her lip. "I don't suppose you have something that could sweeten the deal for them."

"Apart from me not getting Nico to hunt them all down and kill them?" Gio seemed to consider the request. "There was an old law that I'm willing to reinstate where they can serve as privateers to the Republic and where we are willing to turn a blind eye to any deeds carried out against ships that are not a part of the Republic. How's that?"

Sophia grinned. "You don't want to know about it if they aren't attacking our people?"

"Precisely. That is my final offer," Gio replied and turned his gaze to Nico. "You will accompany her as an escort while she delivers this message."

Nico tried to hide his grin. "Of course, my doge."

"And do stay back after this meeting, Sophia. I have some scales for you to stand on," Gio said before following up on the next order of business.

After the meeting was done, Nico and Sophia stayed behind as promised.

"This way, please," Gio said, and they followed him to his office. A small man in a black suit was standing beside a set of scales.

Sophia looked at the scales with a mischievous grin. "I hope all the pastry I've been eating in the past few days counts for something," she said, patting her tummy.

The man introduced himself as Gio's personal representative from the finest bank in Venice.

"The doge has said that you would prefer gold, *signorina*. Would you prefer bars or ingots?" he asked.

Nico had never seen someone as happy as Sophia the moment she stood on the scales and the numbers were written down in the man's small book. He gave Sophia the details of her new account in a leather folder stamped with the bank's seal.

Gio watched it all with an amused look on his face. When the little man was finished with the details, he picked up the scale, tucked it under one arm, and with a deep bow, he left them.

"I can't believe you actually went through with it," Sophia said, a small laugh escaping her.

"We need you to know we keep our promises," Gio replied. "Congratulations on your mating too."

"How did..." Nico began but stopped at Gio's brow lifting. "Thank you."

"I'm glad you decided to do it, despite the circumstances. Although, mating seems a volatile endeavor at the best of times."

Sophia laughed softly. "Mating isn't something that can be denied, even when you can't shift apparently."

"I've seen it denied before." Gio's expression shuttered entirely, all traces of humor gone. "But I suppose that was a long time ago. Please look in on Arkon, Sophia. I know he is very keen on your plan regarding the Varangian mage."

"What plan?" Nico asked.

"Of course, my doge." Sophia bowed low, and somehow still

made it look cheeky.

Outside Gio's office, Arkon and Zahir were engaged in an argument of low whispers and too many hand gestures.

"Has something happened?" Nico asked. Could he not have a day off? He just wanted one boring, normal day.

"No, no. Zahir just doesn't want to believe me when I explain the magic that was powering that sonic weapon," Arkon said, his brows pinching together. "I've been over it and over it. I'll test the powder again, but I know that I'm right."

"It's barbaric! I haven't seen that kind of horror for centuries, and if your Wolf Mage is behind it? She's off the rails entirely," Zahir argued back.

"It's not the Wolf Mage's magic! I know the taste of her power, and this is all wrong," Arkon insisted and then blinked a few times as if finally realizing Nico and Sophia were there.

"I feel like I'm missing something," Sophia said.

"Bones! It's bone dust in the machine, and the magic in it is acting as a kind of battery," Arkon said and pulled at his hair. "It's fascinating."

Nico's stomach lurched. "It's disgusting."

"That too," Arkon replied.

"I tried to tell you that there's other magic being used through harvesting magical creatures," Sophia said. She tugged on Arkon's sleeve. "We need to ask the bastard in the basement what this is about. I promise you, sorcerer, I can get him to talk."

"I suppose this is the plan Gio was referring to?" Nico asked, crossing his arms.

"It's a brilliant plan, and I will be fine doing it," Sophia replied before looking at Zahir. "Are you any good at glamors?"

"Of course I am, *habibi*," Zahir said, chucking her under the chin. "What did you have in mind?"

Nico smacked his hand over his face when he heard the details, but Sophia just raised her chin and glared at him until he gave in. It was going to be another interesting night.

CHAPTER TWENTY-SEVEN

S ophia had seen her share of dungeons over the years, but there was something about the darkness under the doge's palace that swept a chill down her spine. It was like all the opulence on the floors above was a gilded boot bearing down on you. The marble of the floors was warped from the thousands of damned feet that had walked across them.

The manacles itched against her skin, and she tried to remind herself that she wasn't really arrested. Zahir had also glamored her face to look like she had a black eye and a busted lip. Nico had a grip on her bicep as he led her past the cells with a stony expression.

"Stop shoving me, you asshole," Sophia snapped, trying to pull away from him.

"Then keep moving, pirate. You've caused me enough problems," Nico replied in his ice-cold bastard voice. He opened the door to a cell and shoved her inside. "Here, I thought you might like some company on your last night on earth."

Sophia stumbled into the small cell, and Nico slammed the

door behind her. She swore and shook out her manacles in frustration. Her eyes focused on the mage through the bars of the adjoining cell. He looked dirtier than she'd last seen him, but a month in prison would do that to a person.

"I see they finally caught you too," he said in a bitter voice.

"Hello, Vlad. Fancy meeting you here," she replied and walked over to the bars.

"Things didn't go as planned, but these things happen. I can't believe the Silver Serpent finally caught you," Vladek said, moving over to join her at the wall of bars separating them. He looked gaunt and hollow-eyed, but he still was unbroken.

"Oh, I let him catch me." Sophia reached into her boot and pulled out a small flask. "They never think to check a lady's boots." She opened the flask and had a sip. Arkon assured her it was harmless, just lightly enchanted vodka that would loosen a tongue. She was careful to look like she had swallowed a lot more than she did. She held it out to Vladek. "Sip?"

"You're not half bad for a pirate," Vladek said, taking the flask from between the bars. "Why did you bother getting caught?"

Sophia smiled. "Money, my dear fellow. I'm here to get you out."

Vladek choked on the vodka. "Impossible."

"Not so. People already knew I got you into the city. My reputation has been booming after that prank," Sophia said and pulled a pin from her hair. She started to pick the locks on her manacles. "I have been commissioned by the Wolf Mage herself to get you."

Vladek drank from the point. "I don't believe it. Zarya hates me."

"Not anymore. Apparently, she and Emperor Arkadi have gone their separate ways. Big fight, not sure what it was about though," Sophia said, not looking at him as she focused on the cuffs. It was the first time she had ever heard the Wolf Mage being called Zarya.

"I knew she would leave him after she found out about the camps. I tried to tell him," Vladek replied. "Zarya Verasha is nothing if not *honorable*. She got her magic the hard way and doesn't like cheaters either."

Sophia got the first manacle off and shook out her wrist. "What are they like magic camps or something?"

Vladek snorted. "Yes and no. They are where they are teaching bone magic."

"Hmmm never heard of it."

"I don't suppose it's a practice that would be necessary in the Republic." Vladek laughed bitterly. "Arkadi wanted mages that were loyal, so he got his favorite soldiers to start imbibing magical compounds to see if he could make them gain power."

"Is that what you did?" Sophia asked, her mouth dry. The thought of eating bones for magic sent her stomach churning. She had heard stories about it, sure, but she didn't think it was common, or that there were whole camps dedicated to it.

Vladek snorted in disgust. "No. I was already proficient when I went to the emperor and offered my services. It was a risky move, but he needed to see that he wouldn't win this war without magic. Zarya was his only one—his saint—but she's not enough. He needed hidden mages, people who could work in the darkness so that his precious Zarya wouldn't get her hands dirty."

"She's been using battle magic against the Republic for years. Her hands are hardly clean," Sophia scoffed. It was good to know the truth enchantment was working on the Varangian despite the fail-safe built into his mind.

"Zarya is a force of nature. One that Arkadi thought he could control. If she has left him, then the empire is in for turmoil."

"Why do you say that? I saw the amazing ships they are building. The empire is doing just fine."

Vladek shook his head. "No, you don't understand. Church and State go hand in hand in the empire. Arkadi is the State, but

Zarya is the Church. She's been built up to be a living saint, and the common people worship her. It will cause utter chaos if those two are fighting. I don't know why she would want my help or have me on her side. She knows I can't betray Arkadi."

"Everyone can be bought," Sophia said and freed her other hand.

"No, you don't understand. I took a vow to serve him. There's no breaking a blood spell like it."

Sophia grinned. "She's the fucking Wolf Mage, Vlad. I'm sure she's up to the challenge. I mean if she's willing to fight with the emperor, she knows her shit. She's called the Scourge for a reason."

Vladek paced up and down the cell. "Scourge or not, she would've been smart enough to leave her base in Kyiv by now."

"And go where? Her agents found me in Corfu and hired me, but I didn't see her," Sophia said.

"She's a wolf. She will go wherever she feels safest, or she will hide where no one else will look."

"If I was the emperor, I would be kissing her ass as quickly as I could so she wouldn't leave me," Sophia replied. She didn't know how far she could push him.

"Arkadi doesn't know how to kiss ass or apologize. One of the reasons he was trying to make more mages was a fail-safe against her," Vladek said with a soft laugh. "He's already got a team of mages trained specifically to take her down. The bones and blood of other magic users and shifters just super charge their abilities. They always need more, so they made the camps."

He said it so matter-of-factly, like he wasn't speaking about a human slaughterhouse at all. Sophia had never seen someone so devoid of empathy before.

"I suppose that's where all those slaves from the Republic ended up, right? The camps?"

Vladek's eyes narrowed. "Why do you care? I thought you hated Venice."

"I don't care. People need to make money in this world, and I can't judge how they do it," she said with bile creeping up her throat.

"At least in the camps they have a use and a purpose. The Republic should thank us for taking care of their rabble," Vladek replied. "If Zarya wants me out of here, it will be to either kill me or try and get me to join with her."

"As long as I get paid, I don't care what trouble you two get into," Sophia said. She reached through the bars of the door and picked the lock. She really needed to tell Nico that these cells were too easy to get out of.

"What's the plan to escape? This cell nulls my power," Vladek said.

Sophia smiled at him. "You wait here for me. I just need to take care of a few minor details and make sure our escape boat out of here is in place."

"Don't get caught, pirate. I've had enough of the doge's hospitality."

Sophia gave him a big wink, her stomach all acid with everything he told her. "I'll be right back." It was hard for Sophia to walk away. She wanted to wring the bastard's neck. Nico was waiting for her outside of the main doors to the dungeon.

"Are you okay?" he asked, sensing her mood.

Sophia crashed into him, and he hugged her tight. "I want to kill him."

"That good, huh? Did you get anything useful for Arkon?" Nico asked, rubbing her back in gentle circles.

"I did, but I only want to talk about it once. It's too... It's horrible," Sophia replied. Now that the adrenaline from the trick was wearing off, all she felt was nauseous and heart sore.

"We are all meeting at Dom's place for some dinner. They are already there," Nico told her and wrapped an arm about her shoulders.

Sophia hung on to him. "Don't let me go, okay?"

"Never." He gave her a smile that sent warmth back through her chilled bones. "I thought you knew by now there's no getting away from me, sea rat."

CHAPTER TWENTY-EIGHT

Nico had never seen Sophia so withdrawn. She was so pale when she came out of the cells, he wondered if Arkon had accidentally poisoned her.

Dom's house in San Samuele was a warm, welcoming sort of place, filled with beautiful art that he had collected and Stella had painted. He hoped that with Sophia's help, he might make his own palazzo feel like a home again as opposed to a tomb of old memories.

Stella opened the door and beamed at them. It was hard to look at her the same way after the battle. Nico would never forget her wielding lightning as if she was a goddess of thunder.

"About time you turned up! I'm starving, and Antonio wouldn't let me eat until we were all here."

"Who is all?" Sophia asked. Her scent got a little nervous, so Nico gave her hand a squeeze.

"Only the usual troublemakers—us, Arkon, Zahir, and Ezra," Stella said, leading them into the dining room where they were all drinking Dom's good taste in wines and snacking on charcuterie that Anton had placed out for them. The house smelled like warm spice and good cooking from the kitchen. Nico's stomach rumbled. If he thought he had any chance of success, he would have stolen Antonio away from Dom in a heartbeat.

"How did our nefarious pirate fare?" Zahir asked, pouring wine for them both.

"Better than I thought, unfortunately." Sophia downed the wine and took Nico's and finished it too.

"Perhaps we should eat first," Ezra said kindly, taking Sophia from Nico and giving her a side hug. "Antonio has made you gelato because I told him how much you like it."

"Thanks. I could do with some," Sophia said. She sat down next to Arkon and put her head on his shoulder. "You owe me big time, sorcerer."

Arkon patted her head. "You will make a good raven."

"She's not becoming a raven," Nico grumbled and sat on the other side of Sophia. He wasn't so jealous that casual affection would bother him, but he drew a line at espionage.

"Honorary raven," Arkon whispered, making Sophia grin.

She straightened up as Antonio began to bring in steaming plates of chicken cacciatore, fresh, crusty bread, and mounds of butter.

He gave Sophia a bright smile. "It's a delight to meet you, *Signorina* Osara. I have heard so much of your adventures," he said.

Sophia waggled her brows at him. "They are all true, I swear."

After they had eaten and Sophia had been set up with a bowl of gelato, she declared she was ready to tell them about her time in the cells. Nico put his arm around her, her distress already scenting the air.

"The guy is unhinged. I'm going to put that out there," Sophia began. "I said that the Wolf Mage was fighting with Arkadi, and he started talking about the camps that had been set up. They..." Sophia put down her spoon in her gelato bowl. "From what I could gather, they are death camps. Magic users and shifters are being sent there for them to kill and harvest for their bones and blood."

Nico burned with fury and horror as she told them about the mages enhancing their magics, of how they were trained to kill the Wolf Mage if she got out of hand. Arkon's frown deepened with every word she said.

"I *knew* the last few attacks weren't her. The magic was wrong and vicious. It explains why it was bones charging the sonic device." He leaned forward and rested his forearms on his knees. "I still don't know how it works entirely."

"Give it to me," Ezra suggested from her place in Zahir's lap. "If I can't figure it out, I will ask Frederico to help. You don't have to do this all on your own, Arkon."

"I know, I know." He looked back at Sophia. "Anything else?"

"I wasn't sure if you already knew, but he told me her name is Zarya Verasha," Sophia said.

A smile of pure joy crossed Arkon's face. "I didn't know that. How fucking perfect."

"Should we be worried about how happy he is right now?" Dom asked, black brows raised.

"You don't understand. The Wolf Mage's real name has been a carefully guarded secret," Arkon said, getting to his feet to pace.

Nico was starting to worry even more about how manic Arkon was and how his energy seemed to be increasing despite all the battle magic and sleep deprivation.

"She's not going to be silly enough not to have shielding magic active. You won't be able to track her even with her real name, *habibi*," Zahir said. His green eyes flashed with power. "But maybe it's worth a try. It will all depend if she's really left Arkadi at all. This could all be soldier gossip."

"The Wolf Mage is a symbol, and they truly believe she is a saint. They wouldn't make up lies about her for entertainment," Sophia argued.

"Fuck the Wolf Mage," Stella said, throwing up her hands. "We need to find those fucking camps. I have a massive folder of all the victims that have ended up in those places. My best friend was almost sent to them. I won't be able to sleep at night until we try and rescue who is left." Her words came out as a sob, and Dom gathered her in his arms.

Nico had been there the day they had found the ships transporting the unregistered magic users. He never could have imagined that they were being sold off like cattle to a butchering yard.

"If Arkadi really has a group of assassins trained to kill the Wolf Mage, with any luck she's dead already," Arkon said, his mind only ever on one thing. Zahir smacked him in the back of the head. "Okay, fine! I will try and find her. I'll get the ravens hunting down the locations of the camps."

"Vladek seemed to know about them. Perhaps it's time you let me have a run at that psychic wall of his," Zahir said, malice burning in his eyes.

"Whatever you do, we can't let him go free for any deal. You should have seen him talk about the mages eating bones. He didn't have any humanity in him," Sophia said, rubbing at her biceps.

Arkon smiled at her. "You've done very well. We can take it from here, pirate. You have another job for Gio to take care of."

Sophia's nosed crinkled. "Me. Job. It feels so gross just saying it out loud."

"Better get used to it, my mate. You're part of the Republic's trusted council now," Nico teased, pressing a kiss to her temple.

"Don't remind me," she complained.

"Think of the perks."

Sophia grinned at him and fluttered her lashes. "Maybe you need to remind me of what they are again."

"Stop being gross. We have bigger things to worry about," Arkon said, tossing a cushion at them.

"Actually, *you* have bigger things to worry about. I'm taking my mate home to make the most of the two-day shore leave before we are back on a ship," Sophia declared, getting to her feet. They thanked Dom and Stella for hosting and Antonio for cooking before they got in their boat.

"Do you really think they will be able to find the camps?" Sophia asked.

Nico nodded. "Arkon has been obsessed with the Wolf Mage for years. This information not only justifies what he's been saying recently about the change in magic, but you have given him the one thing he's not been able to get—her name. He won't stop until he finds her now."

"Sounds like someone I know," Sophia teased and kissed his throat.

Nico laughed softly. "Are you referring to yourself right now? Because you were obsessed with me long before I knew who you were."

"I just had a hilarious thought. What if Arkon is mating too?" Sophia started laughing, but Nico didn't. "Oh, come on, it was a joke."

"I'm just terrified at the thought of those two ever being in the same room as each other," Nico replied with a shake of his head.

Sophia crawled into his lap. "We turned out okay, didn't we?"

"Better than okay, sea rat. I don't suppose I could convince you to fuck me wearing that crown again when we get home?" he asked, nibbling at her full bottom lip.

His beautiful mate's grin was pure mischief as she whispered, "You'll have to catch me first."

A WOLF IN ASHES

Far to the south, a silver wolf padded through the hills around Rogotin. She was sore and tired from running. Always running. She had been heading west until she heard of a sea battle spoken about in hushed whispers. It was a tale of ships and serpents, of lightning splitting the sky and of a dark sorcerer turning the world red with fire.

The wolf had to see what the truth was for herself.

No one noticed the wolf as she slipped between houses in the dead of night. If they crossed her trail, they would marvel at the frosted footprints she left behind.

The fortress guards were vigilant, but with the charm around her neck, they didn't see the large beast slipping past them and into the charred remains of the tower.

One sniff of her wolf senses and her heart started to gallop at the familiar magic. *He* really had been in the battle. He had never been sent to a battlefield or placed at such risk before! What had they been thinking? The wolf shook off the annoyance she was feeling.

He was her enemy. He was her equal in power, and for years,

187

they had been playing a game of magical chess, pitting will and power against each other.

The wolf's paws smeared the ashes under her before she leaped out of the broken door. She needed to exact revenge on the people who had betrayed her and were ruining her country, and there was only one person she hoped would help her get what she wanted.

She headed north once more. She knew where she needed to go, where the twisted weavings of her wyrd were always leading her. To him. Always to him.

The Grand Sorcerer of the Republic was about to get a visit he never expected, and the world wouldn't be the same again.

ABOUT THE AUTHOR

I am a Finnish-Australian writer that is obsessed with magical wardrobes, doors, auroras and burial mounds that might offer me a way into another realm. Until then, I will write about fairy tales, monsters, magic and mythology because that's the next best thing.

Want to say hi? You can find me on Instagram, or get all the latest news by subscribing to my blog newsletter at: https://amykuivalainenauthor.com/blog-2/

Or Follow Me on Amazon if you would like an email every time I have a new release!

Thank you so much for reading **King of Cups!** If you enjoyed it, please consider leaving a short review or a rating on Amazon, as it helps other readers find my books and means the world to me.

If you are eager for another story filled with fantasy, romance, myth and legend, please keep reading for a sample of 'Wolf of the Sands.'

WOLF OF THE SANDS

1.

Fenrys Rune-Tongue opened her mouth to the sky and let the rainwater drip slowly down her parched throat.

It had been four days since she had been tied to her corner of the longboat. She had lived off the little rainwater she could manage to get into her mouth or suck off the wooden railing she was tied to. Her captors didn't care if she died; they were hoping she would save them the headache of handling her.

In the dark of midnight, the raiders had beached their boat in the bay at her village of Visby, the place of sacrifices, where women came to learn to be seiðr to serve the gods. No one had ever dared attack them. Not until Egil had managed to convince his men it would be easy picking.

Fen had made it harder for them than they expected. She had been trained as a shield maiden and a seiðr, and she had killed seven of the raiders before they managed to overpower her.

It had been sufficient time for the acolytes and the teachers to get away and hide in the forest, and that was enough for Fen.

"We should push her over the side and be done with it," Brandr spat as he glared at her.

Fen smirked. She liked that he was scared of her.

Good.

She was a seiðr, a keeper of stories and magic, a seer and sacred servant of Freya and Odin. Their mistreatment of her was enough for even the strongest of the raiders to be nervous. Egil only laughed at him.

"Don't be a coward. She can do nothing to us without an ax in her hand."

"The seiðr have magic. Who knows what curse she will bring down on us," Brandr argued, earning Egil's fist in his face.

"Shut up. We will be in Hedeby tomorrow, and we will sell her like all the rest."

Fen laughed. "You think anyone is going to buy a seiðr? They will be too scared of the All-Father's wrath as you should be," she said calmly. Brandr raised his fist to her, but Egil caught his arm.

"Leave it. Don't let the witch provoke you," he said. "We are going to sell her to someone who doesn't care about the gods or what powers she might have."

Fen ignored them, settling deeper into her damp blue cloak that still smelled of pine smoke and blood. She tried not to listen as the other female slaves were assaulted that night, as they had been every night since their capture.

She prayed softly to Freya that they would be strong and those who touched them would die screaming and without glory. If she had a chance to get free, she would give them that death for everything they had done.

The goddess's warm presence caressed her, and Fen whispered her gratitude. She was Odin-marked, after all, so the goddess rarely acknowledged her, but Freya was the mother of all seiðr; maybe she would not forget her daughter like Odin had. Fen had saved as many of her priestesses as she could. Perhaps that made Freya look favorably on her.

Fen wanted to know what the fuck the All-Father was

playing at, letting an ox-like Egil take her as a slave. She should have seen their attack in the runes, should have been able to read this journey in her wyrd.

No one had seen it, and that was bad for all of the seiðr.

* * *

The following day, Fen woke to the smell of smoke and a fog so thick, she could barely see the front of the boat. She did her best to wipe the frost off her braid, still stained with blood and mud despite the rain that had been falling on her for days.

As the sun warmed, the fog began to vanish, and the trading port of Hedeby rose out of it—an island of moored boats, raiders, farmers, whores, and foreigners.

"Finally, we can be done with you," Brandr snarled as he directed one of the men to untie her. He wasn't about to lay a hand on her despite his words.

With cramps racing up and down her legs and back, Fen climbed from the boat and onto the wooden jetty to stand with the other twenty slaves. They all looked ashen and not worth the coin Egil would charge for them.

"Walk," Egil commanded, shoving at Fen with the butt of his spear. He wasn't brave or stupid enough to get too close, either. One wrong move, and Fen would have that spear so deep in his gullet that it came out of his throat.

The slaves were herded along the stinking streets, through the fish markets, and where farmers were selling crops. The ring of a blacksmith's forge sounded in the distance, and people were busy selling or buying everywhere. There were also traders from the east—men in richly colored robes selling spices, dyes, and fabrics.

The stench of human suffering, blood, and shit filled Fen's nose as they made it to the slave markets. Women and children were chained in pens, separate from the men, and ranked only slightly higher than livestock.

Fen ground her teeth together at the curse biting at her tongue. She made to follow the women into a pen, but a round shield shoved her back.

"Not you, witch. We would never sell you to this crowd," Brandr said, sharing a smile with Egil. He took the rope of her leash and tugged her along.

There were only the two of them. She would only need a slight distraction. Fen froze as the cold, sharp tip of a spear rested on the back of her neck.

"Don't even think about it. You already cost me seven *vikingar,* and if you weren't worth the gold I need, I would gut you right here," Egil snarled softly. "Now, move."

Fen kept walking, following Brandr and trying to stay out of the way of the crowd. They headed out of town and up a grassy hill.

She wondered if she was being taken to be sacrificed, but no one would pay raiders gold for that, and no one would dare to sacrifice a seiðr.

Cages had been built at the top of the hill, but of metal, not wood. They were filled with criminals and those too dangerous to sell at a regular slave market.

Those hard-faced men all looked like they were going to piss themselves. The slave traders didn't look much happier.

Blank-faced women of all ages were crowded into another cage. Fen couldn't help but notice they were holding up better than the men.

What in Hel's name is going on here?

The caw of a raven made Fen's head snap to the side, and her stomach filled with ice. She hadn't been afraid before, but she was now.

Two stone obelisks rose out of the earth like teeth, strange runes carved into them. They were at least ten feet tall, and sitting on top of each one was a raven watching her.

A Sky Bridge.

She had never seen them but heard the stories and knew to fear them.

All-Father, what did I do to displease you? Fen begged. Surely not something terrible enough to deserve this. She had saved the other seiðr. She had always served the gods loyally. Despite her heartbreak, she would show no fear.

"Good, we made it before they got here," Egil said with a laugh at Fen.

"They are watching us," Brandr whispered, noticing the birds.

"Shut the fuck up. This will be done with soon," Egil replied. "Their gold spends as easily as any other's. The bridge only opens once a year, so any curse for taking the witch will leave when she does."

A pale light began to glow between the pillars, growing brighter as it filled the space. A bronze metal head shaped like a monstrous cat appeared through the light, followed by the rest of an armored body. Four others appeared, all bigger than ordinary men, carrying wickedly curved sickle swords at their sides and shields almost as tall as Fen was.

"You will sell me to the People of Sand and Sky? Do you really not fear the gods, Egil?" Fen demanded, a last pathetic attempt to save herself.

Egil only laughed. "Bitch, the gods won't hear you once you go through the Sky Bridge. Not even Odin himself will be able to see you or hear your prayers."

Fen straightened to her full six feet of height, making the two shorter men step backward in fear of the giantess.

"I pray to Odin that you both live long lives, and you die old men, alone by a hearth and with no honor," she cursed. "You will not see the halls of Valhalla. You will freeze in the wastes of Hel's halls, and no one will remember your name."

Brandr hit her, fear making his face white. Fen tasted iron as she smiled at him and spat on the ground, sealing her curse with blood.

"It doesn't mean shit," Egil said, joining the other traders and the strangely armored men.

"Take it back," Brandr hissed.

"Never," Fen replied, her red-stained smile widening further. Egil whistled at them, and Brandr dragged her forward and thrust her rope at the bronze soldier.

The eyes of the helm were completely black, but Fen could feel them assessing her. A gloved hand touched her long, golden braid, and the warrior nodded. Gold ingots changed hands, and Fen's rope was tied to the train of the other slaves.

The ravens hadn't moved from the top of the glowing Sky Bridge, black eyes watching every moment.

"Why?" she whispered, but no reply came to her. There was no warmth of magic in her fingers or the iron and honey taste of runes on her tongue.

The train of slaves began to move through onto the bridge. As Fen's feet stepped into the burning light, the last thing she knew of Midgard was the black eyes of the ravens and the cold certainty that Odin had abandoned her.

* * *

Need more Fen? 'Wolf of the Sands' is available now!